Jivaro Kill
Robert L. Hecker

To my little sister,
This one is a little
different. Hope you like
it.
                    Bob

Jivaro Kill
Copyright © 2003 Robert L. Hecker

A Double Dragon Press Book

Published by
Double Dragon Publishing
PO Box 54016
1-5762 Highway 7 East
Markham, Ontario L3P 7Y4 Canada
http://www.double-dragon-ebooks.com

ISBN: 1-55404-078-7

A DDP First Edition August 31, 2003

Book Layout and
Cover Art by Deron Douglas

Jivaro Kill
Robert L. Hecker

PROLOGUE

In the gloom beneath the towering trees the forest was so silent that the rare shafts of sunlight seemed only splashes of reality at the edge of the spirit world. The gods had brought down water as they did at the time of the most heat, and the foliage was spangled with shimmering droplets that, to Watakateri, seemed like the watching eyes of *muisak* souls. As the Jivaro warriors slipped through the jungle silent as wraiths their skin was so bathed with sweat that they experienced no discomfort from contact with the wet leaves.

When the water stopped falling the birds come out and began talking to their gods. Watakateri wondered how many of the voices were birds and how many were avenging *muisak wakani* doomed to haunt the jungle throughout eternity. Unlike some snakes, spiders, and larger animals, or even trees which could fall, *muisak* souls in birds could not kill their enemies so they could be ignored. He hoped that if he was ever killed his *muisak* soul would not return in the form of a bird. Or a spider. The idea filled him with dread. A Jaguar or a snake like a Bushmaster would be the only forms acceptable for a warrior.

Watakateri clutched his blowgun and his spear tighter and slowed his steps so he would be closer to the shaman, Marawe, who was walking behind him. If a *muisak wakani* began to hurl invisible soul-killing darts at him the shaman could intercept them and hurl his own mystical darts.

A thought struck Watakateri with a flash so unusual it raced through his body, freezing him in mid stride. Was it possible that your avenging soul would come back as the thing you thought you were when you were alive? The idea pleased him. In his mind he had always been a Bushmaster: sleek, deadly, stalking his unsuspecting enemy, then striking with the speed of a blowgun dart.

The thought was pushed aside by a sudden horror. The Chullachaqui was powerful. If it killed him today, would it also destroy his soul? He must not allow that to happen. Finding and killing such a monster would greatly strengthen his *arutam wakani,* perhaps making his acquired soul so strong he would be immune to death. Then he could return to his home and drink enough *nateema* to make the passage back into the real world where the demons could be held at bay by his powerful *arutam* soul.

He wished he had drunk *nateema* before they left the village. But in this world where the Chullachaqui lived it was not good to drink the fermented juice before the hunt. The darts from his blowgun must speed fast and true or the Chullachaqui would kill him no matter how powerful his *arutam* soul.

A pulsing beat vibrated the moist air and Watakateri halted, holding up his hand so the others would know he had heard and that his ears were still young even though the rest of his body had known many years. Indeed, he should have been killed long ago by someone avenging one of the many enemies whose life he had taken, except that he had been too clever and his *arutam* soul had grown so strong that his enemies were afraid to try. Everyone knew that unless he was killed by a spirit hurling darts or by someone without a soul he would live until one of the gods took him. Still, he was careful when going on a hunt to take the warriors who had killed at least one enemy. Especially when they were going to hunt a Chullachaqui, whose terrible voice now made the leaves tremble.

He did not want to go closer. He did not want to look upon the fearsome creature. But how else were they to kill it and the white men who were its masters? But the power of his *arutam* soul was great. Perhaps even the Chullachaqui could not kill him. He would lead the way to show the others that he was not afraid.

But he was afraid. And the closer they came the more he felt the pounding in his heart, for now he could hear the beast clawing at the forest, making the largest trees fall with a crash that shook the ground. He glanced behind him and saw that even Marawe's face looked tight. And this should not be. Not for a shaman who had the power to speak with Kamari, who could summon the god from the outer world to turn aside the spirit darts when enemies hurled them into his soul.

Then he saw it! His heart thudded like the savage drum beat of a *hanlsamata* dance. The beast with its huge protruding teeth would even frighten a witch doctor. It was roaring, belching smoke, as it hurled itself at the tangle of undergrowth. When it encountered resistance it roared even louder, sometimes backing on its strange rollers before making a new charge. It was more dreadful than he had dreamed in his deepest *campi* death when his soul was separated from his body and roamed the other world. He shook his head. There was a white man riding on the back of the Chullachaqui. The beast was doing the white man's bidding as he pulled and pushed on sticks jutting up from its back. The white man had to have a very strong *arutam* soul. Was he too powerful to kill?

They had to try. And they could certainly kill the other white men who were using machetes and axes to help the Chullachaqui. They should not have come this far. They had been warned. He himself had placed the crossed spears, their points smeared with ampi poison, across the path that other white men had marked through the jungle deep in Jivaro territory. That was two days ago and they ignored the warning, just as those three white men looking for gold had at the time of the most cold and had been killed. It would have been wise to have taken their heads and performed the *hanlsamata* 'soul-killing' dance so their spirits would not come back for revenge. But Marawe insisted that white men did not have souls. And if they did their souls would get lost in the jungle. The white men had no understanding of the transmigration of souls and would not know how to use spirit darts or even make a man sick.

He hoped the shaman was right. He did not like the thought of any man's soul looking for him, even the soul of a white man. It might take refuge in a snake or a big fish and wait for a time when his own soul was weak and susceptible to attack. Since the killings he had drunk much *nijimanche* beer and *nateema* so he would not have to think about it.

This time things would be different. This time they would take the heads of the white men and perform a soul-killing dance no matter what the shaman said. He might even make *tsantsas* out of the heads of wild boars to represent the heads of the three gold hunters and put them with the others so that their souls too would be appeased just in case the shaman was mistaken. If not, no harm would be done, but he would not have to watch so closely for a soul-possessed jaguar or for a tree to fall on him.

He wondered why the Chullachaqui did not sense him and his men. They were well concealed, but a Chullachaqui did not need eyes to see his victims. Perhaps the white man on its back was making it ignore them. Perhaps it was too busy smashing the trees. It never got tired. It was said that it only stopped when the sun dropped low in the sky and the white shaman made it sleep. Then he would climb off its back and the beast would not awaken until the next morning when the shaman again climbed on its back. That would be a good time to attack—when the beast was sleep. He hoped it would not come alive during the attack. But Marawe had assured him that the beast could not come alive without the spell from the white shaman. So if they killed him first, the Chullachaqui would remain sleeping and they could easily kill the others. Except that the white man must be a very powerful shaman to control the beast. Perhaps they should not kill him. With such a shaman in the village none of their enemies would dare attack. Yes, that would be better; if they could do it.

He studied the greenish light that filtered through the canopy of trees, ferns, and vines. Soon darkness would swallow the light. If the tales were true the man riding the Chullachaqui would soon make it sleep. He motioned for his warriors to prepare for the attack, then took a dart from the pouch suspended from his neck by a braided cloth. He pulled a pinch of kapok from the gourd attached to the pouch and twisted the cotton-like fiber around the blunt end of the dart. He wanted this one to fly especially straight. Shooting a shaman was different than shooting any other enemy. Unless he was brought down quickly a shaman could spit demon darts directly into your soul. He also knew that white men usually had shotguns which they kept close when in Jivaro territory. Shaman or not, this one might also have a shotgun. One more reason to shoot his dart very straight. He hoped that none of his warriors would be killed. They would not if they obeyed his command and struck quickly, and together.

A new thought struck him and he grunted, causing the shaman and the husband-of-his-sister crouching nearby to look at him.

"If the white men kill us," he whispered to Marawe above the noise of the beast, "will they take our heads?"

"No. White men do not believe that the spirit of the dead can harm them."

"Even the *muisak wakanis* of their enemies?"

"White men are like women; they have no souls," the shaman said, "so they do not believe that other people have souls."

"Some women have souls," Watakateri reminded him.

"Only if they are very brave." The shaman sounded angry that he should be reminded of something he knew better than anyone. "I have lived among the white men and I know they have no souls, even the brave ones."

That must be true. The shaman had lived in a village of the white men at the edge of the jungle. He had heard that there was a larger village somewhere in the mountains which the white men called Quito. Perhaps there really was such a village. There were so many white men they had to come from somewhere, although why they should want to have the Chullachaqui make a path in the jungle that belonged to the Jivaros he had no idea. Perhaps they too were after gold. That seemed to be the only reason the white men came. They had even entered the territory of the Aucas and the Yaguas, who had killed many of them. Well, after today they would stay in their villages where they belonged.

"Do not kill the one riding the Chullachaqui," he said to the husband-of-his-sister. "He must be a mighty shaman. We can learn from him. Go. Tell the others."

To keep from looking at the clouds of jealousy gathering like angry bees on the face of the shaman he stared at the white shaman riding on the Chullachaqui. He looked very strong, with hair as straight and black as that of any Jivaro. His skin was the same dusky-gold of Watakateri's and his eyes were as dark and piercing as charcoal that held fire deep inside. He looked strong enough to be a warrior as well as a shaman. Still, three darts would bring him down. He would not die if they used the salt quickly. Then they would take him back to their village. If they could learn the secret of his power they could conquer all their enemies.

He felt a thrill of fear as the white shaman made the Chullachaqui lift a fallen tree and fling it aside where other white men began chopping it into smaller pieces. Then the white shaman backed the beast into a cleared area where he made it die, its breath cutting off with a snort of oily smoke. In the abrupt silence the sounds of the other men's axes stood out sharply.

Watakateri checked to see that his spear was close by and that the ampi-coated dart was inserted in his blowgun. He aimed the blowgun through the curtain of vines at the back of the white shaman who was drinking water from a bag that hung from the side of the beast. On either side of him the other warriors placed their spears where they could grasp them quickly and raised their blowguns. He nodded to the shaman who slapped his hands together.

At the sharp explosion of sound the warriors fired their blowguns. The poison-tipped darts blurred across the clearing and thudded into the white men. Watakateri saw his dart hit the white shaman at the base of his neck where it stood out like a miniature flag. For an instant the white shaman thought he had been stung by an insect and he reached back to slap at the dart.

Then he knew! He whirled, reaching up into the beast for a shotgun. But Watakateri's second dart struck him in the arm and he gave up trying to reach the gun. He grabbed a long-handled shovel and stood with his back against the beast glaring at the jungle and yelling in defiance. Watakateri was afraid that the words would awaken the beast and he shot him in the neck with another dart. Then he left his concealment and ran at the man with his spear. He wanted to make him unconscious before he could bring the beast to life. Other warriors came out of the jungle and ran at the white men with their spears. Some of the white men reached their shotguns, but they were killed before they could fire their weapons.

When Watakateri reached him the white shaman was already groggy from the ampi, but he swung the blade of the shovel so hard it made a whistling noise in the air and he had to jump out of the way to keep from being badly cut. Before the white shaman could swing the blade back Watakateri leaped forward, his spear lifted like a club. To his surprise the white shaman brought the handle of the shovel up like a spear and drove it into his side and pain ripped at his stomach as though he had swallowed fire. He doubled and fell back, directly into the arc of the shovel's steel that came around in a vicious blow.

But the blow never landed. The husband-of-his-sister came up behind the white shaman and struck him on the back of the head with the haft of his spear. The white shaman fell to his knees and, with a great force of will, tried to raise the shovel. Again the husband-of-his-sister hit him hard. The shaman's eyes rolled up until they were almost all white and he fell forward on the raw earth with blood welling from the back of his head and matting his hair.

Then the jungle was silent, waiting. All the other white men were dead. Watakateri grunted with satisfaction. They had done well. Not one of his men had been badly wounded, although two or three had been cut by the machetes that some of the white men used to clear jungle growth. Watakateri gritted his teeth against the pain in his side and bent over the white shaman and placed his hand over the man's heart.

"Good. He is alive." The husband-of-his-sister helped him pull the blowgun darts out of the white shaman and rub salt into the wounds to counteract the poison. "Now, everyone will know what it means to be enemies of the Jivaro."

CHAPTER I

Steve Kelly came awake to a familiar odor that brought a welling fear as though the darkness was being dissolved by a carrion breath. Without opening his eyes, he knew! And the horror of where he was drenched him in sweat. What the hell was he doing in a damn hospital? A hospital was where they sent you to die. And even if you failed to die, a hospital meant grinding pain and a forced imprisonment that was worse than pain.

It was fear with a long memory. When he was eleven he had been taken from the clean mountains and forests of Arizona's San Carlos Reservation and placed in a building with cold walls, terrible smells, and people wearing ugly white clothes. And they cut out his tonsils. It had been his first separation from his mother and his home. It had also been his first encounter with the loneliness of fear. They had put him in a ward with sick old people. One of them groaned throughout the night. Only when the light of morning had struggled through the grimy windows was the old man quiet. A short time later, men in white jackets took him away. They never brought him back. For the next three nights as he listened to the moans of anguish and heard the wings of hovering death he promised himself that he would never again be put in a hospital. If he was to die it would be in a place with good memories.

So how did he get here now? He couldn't remember an accident. In fact the last thing he could remember was... Memory exploded with a shock. Oh, shit; those fucking Jivaros. They'd attacked the construction site as he'd shut down the dozer. He was hit by three poisoned darts. He should be dead. A sudden chill shot through him. How bad was he hurt? Oh, God. Blowgun darts...poison. Maybe he was paralyzed.

In a panic he threw aside the sheets and was hit by a wave of nausea and a stabbing pain that made him grit his teeth. It hurt like hell, but at least he wasn't paralyzed. The headache was probably a hangover from the poison. As long as he kept his eyes closed against the stabbing light it wasn't so bad.

He raised his hands to his throbbing head and found that it was swathed in bandages. He must have a head wound. That would account for being knocked out and the headache. He tried to stand.

A soft voice said, "No, *señor. No se mueva, por favor.*"

He opened his eyes. A uniformed nurse with lustrous black hair and warm, dark eyes and an anxious expression gently placed her hands on his shoulders. He allowed her to ease him back on the bed in a semi-reclined position where he closed his eyes and waited for a wave of nausea to pass. He felt a damp cloth being placed on his forehead and he murmured.
"Jesus. Thanks."

"Lie quietly," the nurse said in English. "Quietly, *señor.*"

That was easy. The nausea subsided, but the pain in his head was as sharp as ever. If he moved his brain might explode. His throat was deathly dry, but he managed to croak, "Where the hell am I? What happened?"

"In the hospital," a man said in accented English. "In Quito."
A middle-aged man wearing a white smock was standing beside his bed. The back of the Doctor's thumb was pressed against his lips and his eyes were worried.

"Quito?" Steve whispered. The name sounded familiar, but he couldn't place it.

"In Ecuador."
That's where they'd been clearing the road for the oil pipeline. "Oh, yeah. I remember."

"I am Doctor Hernandez." He picked up a clipboard and held it with his pen poised. "And your name, *señor?* What is your name?"

Steve closed his eyes, fighting panic. What the devil was his name? Why couldn't he remember? Fear began to build. Jesus. Maybe that was it. He wasn't paralyzed; he had brain damage. That was the reason for the pain and the bandages. For some insane reason his social security number popped into his mind. It was instantly followed by a name that he grasped desperately.

"Kelly. That's it. Kelly. Steven J. Kelly." Cool relief swept through him like the mist from a waterfall.

"Very good." The Doctor wrote the name on the pad. "*Señor* Kelly. There are men who would like to ask you, uh, *preguntas*…questions. Do you feel like talking?"

A tingle of alarm sounded. Was he in trouble? Were the men police? If they were, he had to get his facts ready. "What men?"

"From the government. They want to know about your life with the Jivaros."

Steve's head jerked, sending a star-burst of pain through his body. "My what? What's that supposed to mean?"

Dr. Hernandez stared at Steve's face. "You know of the Jivaros."

"The headhunters? Yeah. They made a raid on us." He touched his bandaged head. "I got clubbed…with one of their lances, I think."

"A lance? No, *señor*. Your wound was from a bullet. You have a concussion. You are fortunate to be alive."

Steve remembered the knife-thrust of pain. "Yeah. They got the engineer and the soldiers. Then they came after me."

"Soldiers?" Dr. Hernandez glanced at the nurse who was replacing the damp cloth on Steve's forehead. "When was this?"

What a stupid question. "Yesterday. Wasn't it?"

"What was the date?"

"Who remembers days in that hell hole? All I know is we were clearing roads for the pipeline. We were up along the Napo River when they jumped us."

"I remember that incident. Several men on that road crew were killed."

"You know their names?"

"No. It was…a long time ago."

A long time ago? What the hell did he mean? Steve's hands went to the bandage on his head. It felt clean, new. Something was damn wrong. "How the hell long have I been here?"

Again Dr. Hernandez's eyes flicked toward the nurse. "*Señor*, the pipeline is completed. The raid you were talking about occurred three years ago."

Steve stared at the doctor the pain overridden by stunned disbelief. "Three years?" Was the man trying to tell him he had been gone for three years?

Dr. Hernandez continued to study Steve's face. "You were brought here two days ago after a Jivaro raid on gold prospectors. Two were killed."

It didn't make sense. But why would the man lie? "Those three years…I can't remember a damned thing. You're telling me that I was a prospector?"

The Doctor's face drew into tight lines. "No, you were a Jivaro."

"A headhunter? Impossible!"

"You were dressed as a Jivaro warrior. They said you were using a blowgun quite effectively when you were shot."

"A blowgun? I don't know a damn thing about blowguns."

Dr. Hernandez turned to a white-painted dresser and took a towel-wrapped object from a drawer. "Perhaps this will convince you."

Steve watched in mounting dread as the doctor unwrapped the object. Whatever was in the package, it had to be bad. Hernandez pulled aside the last fold and Steve's gaze locked on the object in fascination. A shrunken human head; slightly larger than a grapefruit with long, black hair. Its skin was wrinkled, almost black, its lips and eyes sewn shut. A 'thing' straight out of a nightmare. But it was human. Or it had been human. And the horror was that Steve recognized it. Somewhere he had seen it before.

"What does that have to do with me?" he breathed.

"You had it tied around your neck on a string. It had only recently been taken."

Steve collapsed back on the bed drained of strength, his mind clawing through a fog of memories. Three years as a Jivaro? There had to be a mistake. He would sort out the truth when he felt better. He closed his eyes and the pain washed over him.

Steve wanted to leave the hospital the next day. But each time he stood up his stomach churned and he grew so dizzy he was forced to return to his bed. He chaffed under the delay. While he was feeling better each day the hospital gave him too much time to rack his brain for answers that refused to come. He had to get back to work. He had to bury the past and plunge into his future before he drove himself crazy wondering how he could have lived with the Jivaros and not remember one thing about it. Amnesia, they called it. Even if it was true, shouldn't there be some fragment of memory in the darkness. But there was nothing. No matter how hard to tried to remember the three years had been wiped from his memory as though they had been removed by the knife of a surgeon.

It was a week before he could stand without feeling as though he was going to toss his breakfast. Still, he moved cautiously as he pulled on a cheap suit that the hospital had provided. It was tight, but that was understandable. Few people in this part of the world were more than six feet tall and weighed close to 200 pounds. He hadn't put on much fat during the three blank years. He actually might have lost a few pounds. God only knows what he'd been eating. His muscles were hard and he moved easily so he must have been getting plenty of exercise. The Jivaros were renowned hunters. Maybe he had gone on hunting trips with them. Maybe even killed people. Maybe take their heads.

He froze. It was possible that he had taken the head himself. He pushed aside the thought. If he had been a headhunter that was one part of his past he hoped he never remembered.

The nurse studied him critically. Her name was Maria and it was she who had made the purchase of his clothes.

"Is okay?" she asked.

Steve moved his shoulders inside the jacket. But not too much. He didn't want to rip the seams. "*Si, querida*," he said. "It'll do."

The anxiety in her eyes was replaced by a mischievous gleam. "You looking...*como si dice...muy guapo.*"

He'd picked up a little Spanish during his months of working for Trans-Am, and there'd been a lot of Spanish spoken on construction projects in L.A., but guapo was new to him. "If you mean big, I guess you're right."

"No, not big, uh, not *grande*. Handsome."

Steve smiled. If she thought he was handsome he was glad he didn't have to see the competition. He was almost ready to leave when Dr. Hernandez came in. Steve had grown to like the diminutive physician during the few days he'd been in his care. He'd become used to the doctor's worried look, which never seemed to change even though Steve knew he was pleased at how quickly he'd recovered from the concussion.

Dr. Hernandez came close to smiling. "Well, I see you received the clothes."

"Yeah, thanks." Steve pulled down the sleeves of the jacket. "I'll pay you back as soon as I collect from Trans-Am."

Dr. Hernandez's frowned. "That might be difficult."

"Why? I've got back-pay coming."

"The pipeline is finished. Trans-America no longer has an office in Quito."

Steve shrugged. "The government owned the company. I'll collect from them."

The Doctor's lips twitched. "You think you can collect money from the government?"

"Okay. Trans-Am's got an office in L.A. I got hired by a guy named Trejo. I'll talk to him."

"It's been three years. He might be there no longer."

"Somebody's gonna pay. They got more than three years out of my life. They owe me."

Dr. Hernandez nodded. "I hope so. You still don't remember those three years?"

"Not a thing."

Hernandez glanced toward Maria as though they shared some secret? "I don't understand how you could survive with the Jivaros, unless…"

He paused and Steve prompted him. "Yeah?"

Hernandez turned his back to stare out the window. "The Jivaros won't touch someone they feel is…*loco*. They feel he is a friend of the Snake Spirits."

Steve smiled grimly. So that's what was worrying them. They thought he might be crazy. "It's something like that with my people."

The Doctor turned to look at him. "Your people?"

"I'm half Apache. Native American."

"Oh, yes. Indio."

"Indian. Right. I grew up on a Reservation in Arizona."

"Ah." Some of the worry went out of Hernandez's face. "That would explain how you were able to survive." He raised an eyebrow. "But the name? Kelly?"

"My father was Irish. He was killed in an accident when I was six. My mother took me back to her people on the reservation."

"Is that where you go now?"

Steve shook his head. "I own a house in Los Angeles. I've got…or I had a girl there."

During the past few days he'd thought about Helen a lot while trying to convince himself that three years wasn't such a long time. His memory of Helen's face and her sunny smile was as vivid as ever. But his conclusion was always the same: three years was a hell of a long time if you were waiting for someone who you probably thought was dead. Most likely she was married and had a couple of kids by this time. Which was one more reason that Trans-Am owed him.

"I see." Dr. Hernandez put his fingers together and held them in front of his lips. "I think it advisable that you remain in Quito for awhile."

"Yeah? Why?"

Hernandez spread his fingers, palm out. "You are still not totally well, let us say. I would like to make more tests."

"No way. There's nothing wrong with me except a headache. I'm going home."

Dr. Hernandez sighed. "I understand. But let me give you the name of a colleague in Los Angeles." He removed a small pad and a pen from inside pocket and jotted a name and address. He tore the page from the pad. "I want you to see him as soon as you are settled there."

Steve folded the paper and slipped it into his shirt pocket. "Yeah, yeah. Okay, doctor."

He didn't want to disappoint Hernandez, but he had no intention of seeing any doctor unless a 16-wheeler used him as a chock. And right now he was doing fine. He was as healthy as he'd ever been. The nagging headaches would go away as soon as the concussion healed a little more. He must have taken one hell of a shot to the head for the effect to last this long. Good think he had a thick skull.

"I'll have to send you the money I owe you."

"No," Hernandez said. "It is paid for by my government."

Steve's lips twitched in a bitter smile. That might be all he'd ever get out of the government. When he got home he'd see Trejo and get his money one way or the other. He picked up the small travel bag they'd given him, which now contained a razor, a toothbrush, a pair of socks, and an extra shirt. Not a hell of a lot to show for three years. Then he remembered that there was one more thing he owned.

"Oh, yeah," he said. "You still got that head?"

Dr. Hernandez looked surprised. "Yes. In my office."

"Can I have it?"

Hernandez spread his hands. "If you wish. But why?"

"It should be worth something. Besides, it looks like it's all I'm gonna get outta this country."

Dr. Hernandez gave him a pained look as though he wished that Steve could take away something better from his country than a shrunken head. As Steve moved to the door he turned to Maria who was biting her lips. She had been good to him and he wished he had something to give her. He'd have to send her something when he got back. Maybe a nice ring or earrings. She'd look good in the long dangly kind.

"So long, *querida*." He reached out to touch her cheek and she cringed. "What's wrong?"

Hernandez said, "It is nothing. Just that some of our people are still afraid of headhunters."

Anger and disgust flooded Steve. What the hell did she think he was? He was no headhunter. She could forget her damned earrings. He stalked out of the room, glad to leave all of it behind: the pain, the worry, the stupid hostility. Things would be okay when he got to L.A.

CHAPTER 2

After twelve years with the LAPD, six as a detective, Lieutenant Henry Warner was used to violent death however Torquemadan, but he had to force himself to look at the body. It was no wonder the woman who called 911 was hysterical. They'd said the victim's name was Trejo, but hadn't said if it was male or female. Identification would be easier if the body had a head. Looking at it he was reminded of a remark by Justice Holmes who had been noted for dissention. When he had been told to look at a flock of newly sheered sheep, he had replied, "At least they're sheered on the side I can see."

Henry assumed that the victim was male because the part he could see was dressed in men's clothing, which didn't mean much these days. It was a dark gray suit with matching vest, expensive to judge by the texture and the lining. The low boots with high Cuban heels were also expensive; snake-skin or, perhaps, lizard. Two hundred dollars, if they were genuine. The necktie had been ripped off and thrown to the side. And the shirt, silk probably, was torn half open to reveal the upper slope of a hairless chest. Not many women would have a chest like that so until he was proven wrong Henry decided that the body was that of a male.

He estimated the man's weight at 180-lbs; height 5'5". He was mildly amused to realize how much a person relied on someone's head to determine their height…and sex. But lately even that was suspect. Without makeup and with short hair, many women could pass for men; or vice versa. Some of the most beautiful women he could remember had turned out to have testosterone hormones that would have made Rasputin proud. In this case, it didn't make a hell of a lot of difference. The body would be just as dead if it was male or female.

He moved as close as he could without stepping in the bloodstain on the thick carpet and crouched to examine the cut. It was low on the neck, likely made with the clasp knife that was lying beside the body. The open blade looked very sharp. Still, the killer had to be strong to severe the spine so neatly. The photographer had finished taking pictures so Henry used his pencil to edge the knife into a plastic evidence-bag. He placed the bag inside a manila envelope, labeled, and sealed it.

He stood up and moved back. A messy job. Too bad that whoever had to clean up the mess couldn't bring in a hose and sluice out the place. He'd seen that done once in a tiled bathroom after a wrist-cutting suicide where the victim hadn't been considerate enough to use the bathtub. But this room was a den, large and comfortable with a fireplace that burned real wood. The furniture was massive, damask-covered, possibly antique. A large desk with gold inlays was angled across one corner, facing the fireplace. The wall paneling had to be real walnut. On two walls bookcases rose from the floor to the beamed ceiling. An ornate chandelier was augmented by expensive-looking lamps. Heavy brocade drapes were pulled back from leaded-glass windows. There were several paintings that looked like Goya or Velazquez reproductions making a nearby lithograph of Messier's 'Jungle' look shockingly garish.

He couldn't help but compare the room with the den in his modest bungalow. This was old money and plenty of it; his was new mortgage and endless payments. There were a few similarities. His den had wall to wall carpeting, but was so worn that in some places the matte showed through. He also had bookcases, only made of adjustable shelves fasted to metal frames attached to wallboard. And instead of a chandelier his low ceiling supported a glass fixture with two 75-watt bulbs. More wattage would trip the old circuit breakers. But his desk was almost as big as this one, only made of steel and topped with Formica and its carpet of papers made it look as though a tornado would be a blessing. He wished he had a real fireplace like this one. But at a buck a log he would have a hell of a time feeling romantic in front of an open fire watching the pennies go up the chimney. Oh, well. The gas furnace in his attic worked fine if you didn't mind the vibration from the cylinder-fan and its rumbling roar.

One other thing: his house was a seventy-year-old, two bedroom bungalow in Altadena; this was at least ten rooms of Tudor-style mansion in L.A.'s fashionable Holmby Hills. Still, his den didn't have blood on the floor. Damn shame about the carpet. It must have cost a fortune; it was doubtful that it could be cleaned. He wondered what kind of a market for there was bloodstained Persian carpets. With so many nuts in the world the stain might even make it more valuable.

He glimpsed himself in a full-length mirror secured to the wall by a massive, ornate frame encrusted with gold-leaf. As usual his mahogany-colored hair was a fright from running his fingers through it. It was thick, thank heavens, with no sign of gray. But it also had a mind of its own. Every morning he tortured it into a part somewhere in the vicinity of the left side. But the hard fought victory never lasted more than ten minutes before, in a burst of rebellion each hair, went its separate way. He had considered using hairspray, but rejected the idea as a sign of defeat. One good thing: the wide-set gray eyes that looked back at him were clear and reasonably intelligent if he squinted just right.

But his posture was terrible. The way he stood with his head thrust forward and his chest concave made his jacket hike up in back. It made him look old. As he straightened he glanced around to make sure nobody was watching. Hell. Thirty-five wasn't old. He still looked pretty good…when he held his shoulders back. He was a shade over six feet, with the slender length and good chest that had made his tailor rub his hands in anticipation the first time he had seen him. He remembered how old Guido had clucked when, in taking measurements, he had detected the hard muscles in Henry's limbs. Guido wouldn't have been so surprised if he knew about the long hours Henry spent pumping iron in the police gym trying to make his muscles bulge like those of the big boys, which they refused to do even though he could match his lifting capacity with most body builders. But there was one advantage to not being built like a gladiator; Guido's clothes looked good on him…when he remembered to stand tall, which was getting harder to do.

What the hell? The LAPD didn't pay you for your looks. When he had first made detective in the Burglary-Homicide Division, the other guys gave him a bad time about his tailor-made suits and jackets. But he pointed out that his customized clothes didn't cost much more than the expensive rags they were buying off the racks after they finished paying for alterations. Besides, on what else should he spend his salary, plus a lot of overtime? He wasn't married. His car was paid for. After fifteen years of back-breaking payments even his house was almost paid for. He didn't date as much as he had before his intellect overtook his hormones. Lately, he hadn't found a girl he considered worth more than a few hours of his time. He was beginning to wonder if he ever would. Romance just wasn't part of his nature. Not that he minded. From what he had witnessed of modern love and marriage it could really foul up your day.

He snorted at his image. Stupido. Life had been a lot more fun before he'd gotten so damn analytical. Maybe that was what was meant by maturing. It had taken him a long time to sort out his own life pattern into orderly segments of work, training and exercise leavened with an appropriate modicum of recreation and entertainment. To some people his life might appear structured and dull, but he liked the order, the security. Changes that upset the pattern were not welcome.

He turned to watch Dr. Eugene Woods, the M.E., examine the body. This case fit neatly into the warp and woof of his life pattern. It was just unusual enough to be intriguing and, apparently, would not require any long trips out of the county.

Woods grunted and stood up, grimacing with the effort. He moved away from the body and pulled off a pair of surgical gloves. Henry waited impatiently while the M.E. took a thick cigar from his pocket, stripped away its container and carefully began the ritual of setting it ablaze. Between billowing puffs as finely timed as a metronome, Woods asked, "Who was he?"

"So it is a he."

"Did you have any doubts?"

Henry grinned. "Just wanted to make sure you're doing your job."

Wood's snorted. "Me? You don't even know his name."

"Sure, I do. Trejo. Rep for a company called Trans-American."

"I've heard of them. Subsidized by the government of Ecuador. This could be trouble."

Henry shrugged. "What isn't? Any idea what killed him?"

Gene Woods drew on the cigar and looked sideways at Henry and said in a voice with all the life of an oak leaf in December, "I'd say getting your head cut off would do the job."

"I didn't mean that. I meant, was that what killed him? Or was he dead first?"

Woods grinned again, causing Henry to wonder what it would take to make the M.E. feel as ill as he was with a knot of bile in his stomach that wanted to come up. That was one part of the job, in fact, about the only part of his job that he didn't like: the occasional really gruesome crime. But as the saying went, half of knowing what you want is knowing what you're willing to put up with.

"Can't tell yet," Woods said. "No wounds on the body that I can see. So whatever killed him must have been in the throat area. We won't be able to tell for sure until the autopsy. Any lead on who did it?"

Henry coughed and waved aside a cloud of pungent cigar smoke. "Nothing yet."

Two men from the coroner's office came in pushing a gurney stretcher. Working carefully, they began putting the body in a body bag.

"Why do you suppose he wanted to cut off the head?" Woods asked.

"Who knows? I've got a better question. What did he do with it?"

Woods waved at a puff of noxious smoke apologetically, "He must have had a use for it."

"What use would anybody have for a head?"

"Oh, witchcraft. Anatomy study." Woods' lips twitched. "Trophy for the mantle."

Henry shook his head, thinking it might be a blessing to have a perverted sense of humor if you were an ME. "What about the time of death?"

"About midnight, I'd say. I can pin it down closer after the autopsy." Henry moved out of the den into the living room where the furnishings were equally elaborate, including two huge chandeliers that hung from the beamed ceiling on massive chains. The rugs looked so expensive he felt guilty about walking on them.

Detective Sergeant Fuller was standing beside a woman who was seated in a fragile chair that could have been a genuine Louis XIV. She dabbed at her eyes with a limp handkerchief. Henry judged her to be in her mid-30s. She was a handsome woman with ivory skin and a mass of dark hair that framed her face. She was buxom without being too heavy. That would come in a few years. She wasn't wearing a wedding ring, although there were plenty of other rings on her pudgy fingers. She reminded him of a dusky rose whose petals were ready to fall. Henry had learned that her name was Carmen Ortega. She was a naturalized citizen from Ecuador and she worked at the Trans-America offices as Trejo's secretary.

"Miss Ortega?" Henry kept his voice dry and professional to help her hold her emotions in check. Ordinarily, he began his interrogations with friendly chatter, then edged into the nitty-gritty. But this woman needed steel more than butter. "Do you have any idea who could have done this? Or why?"

Her dark eyes glistened with tears. "No, no," she murmured.

"Did he have any personal enemies that you know of?" She shook her head, her restless fingers making rosary beads out of the damp handkerchief. "Did he keep large amounts of cash or other valuables here?"

"Cash? No, no. I don't know." Her eyes clouded in anger. "You think it was a ladro…robber?"

"We don't know yet. You came here this morning to find out why he didn't come to the office?"

"Yes. He had an important meeting. He did not come. And I knew he was well last night."

Henry felt a familiar thrill. It was always like that when he sensed that he had detected something he could use. "How did you know that?"

Her shoulders slumped. "I was here. But only to work."

"What time did you leave?"

"At eleven-thirty. About then."

"He was alone then?"

"*Si*. Yes."

The tingle faded. "Was he involved in any…disputes?"

She stared at him, her beautiful eyes wide. "Disputes?"

"Arguments. Ah, altercations. Fights."

"Oh, fights." Her lips twisted into a wry smile. "You don't know our office. We have those every day."

"Oh. About what?"

She lifted her shoulders. "Relatives. Trade transactions. The Columbians are angry because we are selling more goods than they are. The Peruvians are angry because we are not selling enough to them. People are angry because they owe us money, or they say we owe them. Yesterday a man had to be forced to leave the office."

Sergeant Fuller paused in his note taking and raised an eyebrow at Henry. But Henry was already pursuing the sliver of suspicion. "What man?"

"I don't know. He force his way into *Señor* Trejo's office yelling that we owed him money. *Señor* Trejo would not talk to him. He call Manuel and Juan and they put him out...with much difficulty."

"Did he have an appointment?"

"No. He just come in."

It figured. That would be too easy. "And you didn't get a name." He felt like adding "naturally".

"No." She looked up at him through luminous eyes. "You think it was him?"

"I doubt it."

Most murders were not committed by strangers. This would probably turn out to be some sort of a revenge killing because of a woman, although there was always the possibility that Trejo had been involved in a drug operation. Except that dealers didn't call attention to themselves by creating a disturbance in their partner's office.

Even so, he had better follow up. At the moment, it was all he had. "What did he look like?"

She dabbed at her eyes again. "He was Chicano. Big. A big man, more than six feet."

"You mean fat?"

"No, no. Strong. Tough."

"You said Chicano. What made you think that?"

"His face. Black hair. Kind of long. But I do not think he spoke Spanish."

"How do you know that?"

"He did not curse in Spanish like the others. Spanish is very good for the cursing."

"Other? What others?"

"Oh, *Señor* Trejo is threaten every day by somebody. Manuel and Juan are there to throw people out. They are bodyguard, kind of."

Henry felt a dull disappointment. It was too much to expect that he would have a good description of the killer. Correction; possible killer. This murder was bound to have political implications and it would save a lot of time dealing with reporters if they caught the perpetrator quickly. But even if they did there would still be problems. He would have to make dozens of reports for submission to the Ecuador authorities. And if Trejo had so many altercations he had to keep bodyguards it was going to be difficult to track down one unidentified angry man. But part of his job was pulling in all the strings, even if all you caught was hell.

"How was he dressed? A suit...business clothes?"

"No, old jeans and a leather jacket. I think he was workman, a laborer."

"You got that from his clothes?"

"Yes. You could tell that."

Henry wasn't so sure. A few years ago the way a person dressed could be used to categorize his station in life. But today even a millionaire might be wearing beat up castoffs, at least in Los Angeles, home of the laid-back individualist who might wear a ring in his ear because he wanted to be different and drive a BMW so he wouldn't be. One more thing that made his job difficult.

The coroner's men passed, pushing the Gurney with the body bag on it. Miss Ortega's chest heaved until Henry feared that her ample breasts were going to split the fabric of her dress while dry sobs forced their way past the sodden handkerchief pressed against her lips.

Henry motioned Sergeant Fuller aside. "Get a statement from her when you can. See if you can get a better description of that guy from yesterday and anybody else overly aggressive during the last few days. Check with those guys, Manuel and Juan."

"Okay. But if what she said is right it isn't going to help much."

"I know," Henry agreed. "But see what you can do."

He walked outside and stood on the flagstone steps of the big Tudor home. The day had slept well and awakened feeling good. If you could forget what was inside the house it was a day for dreaming. The air was fragrant with flowers. An immense sweep of emerald grass flanked by groomed flower beds snuggled up to a circular drive all the way to a brick wall that circled the estate, broken only by ornamental-iron gates. He wondered if they had been locked last night. Not that it mattered. A strong, agile person could scale the wall. Or he could have slipped through when it was opened to allow the secretary to enter or leave. Too bad the beautiful home had to be tainted by a murder. It might cause the market value to drop a few hundred thousand. Maybe he should make an offer. He might be able to afford the swimming pool.

He snorted in disgust at his whining self-pity. Lately, it seemed that every time he encountered a sumptuous home he found himself wondering if he couldn't have made it big if he had chosen some other profession. Did a former Boy Scout from the wrong side of the San Fernando Valley have the intelligence, the abilities to succeed in a line of work that would generate this kind of money? Well, too late to find out now. He was committed. He was a thirty-five-year-old career detective who was considered good at his job. No genius, but good. And he was in good shape; maybe five pounds on the hefty side. Make that more like ten pounds. But he could take that off in a hurry when he got back to jogging which he had given up during his vacation last year. He would start again next week for sure.

He sucked in another deep breath of the aromatic air. Even an edge of smog couldn't spoil the perfumed sunlight. Maybe it wasn't too late. He could go to college at night. Maybe study law. Or medicine. Half the big homes in the neighborhood were owned by doctors or lawyers. Or politicians. It was never too late to get into politics. If you wanted to sink to that level.

A patrolman came around the corner of the house, his voice excited when he said, "Lieutenant, we found footprints behind some bushes, like the guy was waiting."

Henry put his hand on the patrolman's shoulder. "Good work, officer. What's your name?"

"Robert Austin." Patrolman Austin pointed at a bush with waxy leaves near the front door. "Right there, sir."

"Okay, Austin. Many thanks. Would you go inside and ask Sergeant Fuller to come out here, please?"

"Yes, sir."

Henry stared at the bush that could have concealed a murderer. If there was only some way to make inanimate organisms talk it would certainly make his job easier. The murderer had probably slipped in through the gate when it was opened for the secretary's car. He had watched her go into the house and concealed himself behind the bush until she came out.

When she walked to her car with Trejo the killer had slipped in through the open door and grabbed Trejo when he came back inside. There was no way of telling if he had killed Trejo immediately or if they had talked first.

A patrolman trotted up the curving driveway. "We found it," he said in a too loud voice. "By the gate."

The patrolman's pasty face told Henry what had been found, but he said it anyway. "The head?"

"Yeah."

Henry felt a twinge of regret. There went the exotic element. No psycho would have left without his trophy. Not after he'd gone to so much trouble to get it. Then Henry saw that the patrolman's expression. "What is it?"

The patrolman licked his lips. "We found two."

"Two heads?"

"Yeah. A big one. From the guy in the house, I guess. And a little one."

Jesus. What the hell was going on?

"Show me," he said.

As he followed the patrolman he wondered if the man had made a mistake. There couldn't be two heads. Unless there was another body they hadn't discovered. A small one? Maybe it was that of a child. But why had the killer taken the head if he was going to leave it behind? Maybe he'd changed his mind. Didn't want to get blood in his car or something. But if the killer was insane, he wouldn't need a logical reason. He probably changed his mind every time he burped. There was always the possibility that he'd heard something that had scared him. A car going past? They would have to ask the newspapers to run a message asking for people who had been driving past at the time of death. But the chances were less than nil that anybody had seen anything. If this was a one-time-only revenge killing, they might never find the killer.

The patrolman stopped near the wrought-iron gate where another patrolman was waiting. The man's face was flushed as though his heart was working hard. Revulsion tugged at the corners of his mouth as he pointed to the edge of the driveway.

The first thing Henry noticed was the eyes. They were wide and staring, peering through the leaves of a low bush as though searching for eternity. Looking at the head gave him a curious feeling. Eyes were supposed to be attached to a body. But there was no room for a body beneath the bushes.

"Where's the little one?" he asked the patrolman.

The patrolman pointed to a place just behind the head of Trejo and Henry gasped. It was small, but grotesque; with pinched, ugly features, the lips and eyelids sewn together, long, black hair framing the awful features. Henry had seen heads like that in pictures. It was the shrunken head made by headhunters.

A car from the L.A. Times pulled into the driveway and a reporter got out, followed by a photographer. Henry moved to intercept them. This one was going to sell a lot of papers.

CHAPTER 3

Steve Kelly worked the controls of the Case backhoe mechanically. He had been running backhoes for so many years he didn't have to concentrate on the task as he forced the steel-jawed bucket into the deepening trench, then swung the load of dirt and rock up into the waiting truck. Usually when he daydreamed on the job, it was about a girl. Today was different. Today his palms were slippery and his forehead was pinched into a worried cleft. How had he gotten all that blood on his clothes and his hands? Where the hell had it come from? Where had he been last night?

He probed his memory from some shred of an idea that would lift the edge of darkness. It had to have happened last night. But when? He had gone to the Trans-Am offices in early afternoon. That bastard Trejo had thrown him out; the son-of-a-bitch. He remembered that his head hurt like hell so he had stopped at a bar for a couple of shooters. At home he'd taken a fist full of aspirin and hit the sack. After that, nothing. He'd sleep like a log all night.

So where the shit did all the blood come from? Wait. Something was missing. Dinner. With Helen.

The first day back in L.A. he'd found out that Dave Grady was supervising the construction of a high-rise apartment complex in Eagle Rock. Current headquarters for Grady Construction was in a mobile trailer mounted on jacks near the edge of the site where excavation work was getting underway on the foundations. Good. That meant that Grady might need another heavy equipment operator.

When he'd walked into the construction trailer it was difficult to control his excitement. He wondered if Helen still worked for Grady. Would she be as beautiful as ever? Three years shouldn't make that much difference. Then he relaxed. She would either be married, or hate him. He had walked out on her to take the job in Ecuador. Either way he was out of it.

Dave Grady was standing at the far end of the trailer near one of the barred windows, angling an inventory report so he could read it in the sunlight. Helen sat at the same old battered desk behind the blue-print-cluttered counter punching the keyboard of a computer. Her blonde hair was just as clean and beautiful as he remembered. Her lips, pursed in concentration, were just as sensuous; her waist was as trim; her hands just as slim and white. And there was no wedding ring! Maybe there was a chance.

He kept his face impassive, but his heart pounded when he cleared his throat to catch her attention. She swung the swivel chair and stood up, wearing a professional smile.

"Yes?" At first she didn't recognized him. Then the smile faded and her eyes widened. "Steve?"

He grinned at her. "Hi, baby."

Her face drained of color so quickly he was afraid she would faint. "Oh, my God."

He shoved through the swinging gate in the counter and caught her as her knees buckled. Dave Grady looked up and dropped the report.

"Hey! What the hell are you doin'?"

Then Steve had Helen in his arms and she put her arms around his neck, as she murmured, "Steve. Oh, I can't believe it."

He breathed in the perfume of her hair and savored the feel of her firm back under his palms. How had he ever been able to leave her? He knew he could never do it again. Dave Grady slapped him on the back. "Steve Kelly; you son-of-a-bitch. We thought you were dead."

Grady had been happy to give him a job. Construction in L.A. was far from booming, but experienced rig operators were hard to find. Maybe it was true, but Steve also knew that if Grady hadn't hired him, Helen would have quit. Even now he couldn't believe how happy she was to see him again, all the bitterness burned away by time and worry. And last night they'd gone out to dinner. And after dropping her off at her apartment he'd gone straight home. Hadn't he? So where had the blood come from.

When his alarm clock went off in the morning he was sleeping deeply. He remembered that. He had to force himself out of bed. But that wasn't unusual. Getting up before daylight had never been one of his favorite things even when he'd been a kid on the reservation. Whoever had said that Apaches were early risers was crazy. It seemed that his body had always craved another few minutes of rest.

Since his return from Ecuador getting his body moving in the morning was like forcing his way through a bad hangover. He must be getting old. He hadn't felt this bad even when he used to stay up half the night boozing and raising hell.

Sitting on the edge of his bed he brought his hands up to rub his throbbing temples. That was when he blinked in surprise. His hands were streaked with a black substance. What the hell? He rubbed his fingers together. Dried blood? God knows he'd seen enough of it at one time or another, often his own.

Where in hell had it come from? He hadn't been in a fight. Except for taking Helen to dinner he hadn't gone anywhere. Could he have somehow cut himself while he was asleep? Maybe a nosebleed.

He checked his body for cuts. Nothing. And his nose felt normal. Still, that had to be it. Maybe the change in climate had affected his nasal tissues. It might take him a few weeks to get back to normal.

Thinking of Ecuador brought back a surge of anger. Those sons-a-bitches at Trans-Am weren't about to pay him what they owed. He could take them to court. But shit. That would take months...years. His surge of rage was replaced by a dark despair. He would never get his money. What the hell? Better forget it. He had his old job back and didn't need the money anyway.

Thoughts of the job brought him to his feet with a groan. The damn headaches were draining his energy. It was even an effort to walk to the bathroom.

He pushed open the door and snapped on the light and his breath exploded in a gasp. What the hell was this? His clothes were on the floor where he must have dropped them; spattered with dried blood! His eyes widened in disbelief. There was dried blood and pools of red-tinted water everywhere; on the sink, on the floor. What the fuck had happened? It looked as though he'd butchered a cow.

But somehow he knew the blood was human. And not his own. So whose was it? To lose that much blood the person would have to be dead. But where had he gotten it? Why the hell couldn't he remember? He must have been drunk. No, he hadn't been drunk when he dropped Helen off after dinner. He'd been tired as hell, but not drunk. Shit. He hadn't had more than a couple of beers all evening. But he must have. Why else would he be unable to remember?

Maybe he'd stopped at some joint on the way home. Gotten into a fight. Jesus! Had he killed somebody? Or had he been trying to save somebody's life? Maybe someone had been in an accident and he'd tried to help them. If that was true there might be something about it in the papers. He'd have to check when he got off work.

"Hey, Kelly, you dumb shit! Watch what the hell you're doin'!"

The cry snapped Steve out of his reverie and he saw that the backhoe's bucket had swung too far. Before he could halt its motion it struck the cab of the truck with a solid clang, leaving a fresh scar on the battered metal. A heavy-bellied Chicano with a low forehead, a drooping mustache, and arms like a gorilla glared at him.

"You mother!" Gordo Sanchez screamed. "Look what you done to my cab!"

Sanchez was an independent trucker so he had to pay for any repairs himself. Not that he had ever done so. His Mack 10-wheeler looked as though it had battled half the skip-loaders and backhoes of the world and had lost every fight.

"Sorry, Gordo," Steve called as he swung the bucket away.

"Sorry don't buy crap," Sanchez snarled. "Next time I take your fuckin" head off."

Steve stifled a surge of anger. After all, it was his fault. He should have been paying attention. Too bad it was Sanchez's truck. The big Mexican had a nasty temper, and was always looking for an excuse to use his heavy fists. If there was one thing Steve did not want it was a fight. Sanchez's reference to taking his head off triggered a disturbing image, as brief as a lightning flash, of hands covered with blood using a pocket knife to cut the head off a dead man. Steve's body was cold and clammy.

The men on the construction crew were watching for his response to Sanchez's challenge. A week ago, hell, a day ago, he would have been off the deck and all over Sanchez. But now he had to hold that brief flash of horror, and try to fit it into a time and place. The thought was torn away by the powerful blast of an air horn on a caterer's truck as it wheeled to a dusty stop.

The men hastened to form a line with Gordo Sanchez shoving into a place near the head. Steve shut down the backhoe and went to the end of the line. He bought two plastic-wrapped ham sandwiches and a large cup of coffee. Instead of sitting with the other men in the shade of a White 16-wheeler he found a place where he could be alone in the shade of a load of 1" plastic conduit pipe. As usual, a couple of the stray cats came by for their handout.

As he gave scraps to the cats Steve noticed the way the men looked at him and whispered. They probably thought he was afraid to be near Sanchez. Let them believe what they wanted. He had to try to recapture the disturbing image. There was something familiar about the decapitation. It had to have been a flashback to the years when he was a headhunter. He felt a twinge of nausea. It wasn't possible. He might have become a Jivaro, but he could never cut off anyone's head, dead or alive.

"Hey, hot shot!"

Steve looked up. Sanchez swaggered toward him, pulling on leather work gloves, his heavy features twisted into a scowl. The other men stopped eating. Instinctively, Steve's hand felt for the clasp knife he carried in his pocket, but it was gone and his worry deepened. Sanchez glared down at him, his eyes bright in the thick folds of his face.

Sanchez stared down at Steve, his eyes bright in the thick folds of his face. ""I hear you're part Apache." His growl was loud enough for the other men to hear.

Steve looked up at Sanchez and let his contempt show in his eyes. He took a slow swallow of coffee so Sanchez could see that his hands weren't shaking. "So?"

"Well, Chief, I figure you owe me some wampum or whatever you slops call money."

Sanchez was trying to force a fight. It had been building since the first day Steve started work, ever since the men who knew Steve from jobs in the past had passed the word that he was not a man to fool with. The information was a challenge to Sanchez. It was necessary that he establish his claim as *el jeffe* over the newcomer. The accidental scratch to his truck was just the excuse he'd been looking for.

But Steve could not fight. He had to pursue the flashing image of a dead man before it vanished as had so many images since he'd left the hospital in Quito. He looked at his hands holding the cup of coffee.

"Okay," he muttered. "How much?"

Sanchez's face went slack. Then he grinned at the watching men. "Fifty bucks."

The price was ridiculous. It took tremendous willpower for Steve to reach in his pocket and take out all the bills he had. His hands were trembling as he counted them and that was more disturbing than the act of submission. Sanchez would think it was because he was afraid. He clinched his jaws and held out the bills to Sanchez.

"Here's twenty-three bucks," he gritted. "All I've got."

Sanchez took the money with a puzzled look on his face. Nobody with Steve's reputation as a hard man would roll over so easily.

"I should take the rest of it outta your hide," he said, and took a step forward.

Steve's hand closed around a six-foot length of plastic pipe. It wasn't as heavy as metal, but it would make a formidable weapon in the hands of somebody who knew how to use it. He stared up at Sanchez, letting his contempt and anger show in his eyes.

He said softly so the others couldn't hear, "Let it go, Sanchez."

Steve could almost read his mind. He knew that Steve wasn't afraid of him, so there had to be a reason why he wouldn't fight. It might be better to accept his victory. Hell, you couldn't trust an Indian, especially not the way he was holding that piece of conduit. Sanchez backed a step and held the money up so the others could get a good look at it, then shoved it in his pocket.

"Shit," he said loudly. "I ain't greedy. I'll let you off easy. But next time...fifty bucks a crack." He turned to the others, shifting the emphasis away from Steve so he could walk away. "And that goes for you mothers, too. That rig's too valuable to get all beat up."

Somebody laughed and the others grinned, watching Sanchez's face. When he also laughed, they joined him. Steve let his breath out and relaxed his grip on the conduit. Sanchez would never know how close he had come to having a plastic pipe shoved through his gut like a spear.

A spear? Why had he thought of that? Steve's attention focused on the length of plastic and his mind clicked like a camera shutter. Instead of a hollow conduit he saw a Jivaro blowgun.

The picture vanished, but the feeling that the image was important would not go away. Could it be connected with what had happened last night? No. It was part of those lost years he'd spent with the Jivaros. Dr. Hernandez in Quito had told him that such memory flashes would occur. Those years were buried in his subconscious. Maybe someday he would remember everything. In a way, he was afraid of that. God only knew what he had done. Maybe it was better if those years stayed lost. Besides, they couldn't be connected with the blood on his clothes. Could they?

When Steve headed for home he took the length of plastic pipe with him.

CHAPTER 4

Henry Warner sat at his Formica-topped desk and tried to think positively as he studied the knife without touching it. It was an ordinary clasp knife, about four inches long, with two blades and an artificial bone handle. The longest blade was open. Blood had dried on it, and when Henry had carefully removed it from the plastic evidence bag, a little of the dried blood had flaked off on the desk top. He hadn't bothered to put the flakes back in the bag. There was plenty left for the lab people to do their work. It would all prove to be Trejo's anyway, of that he was certain.

He continued to stare at the knife as though he could mesmerize some drop of information from it. Ordinary. A man's knife. The type you could buy in a million stores in dozens of countries. Or order from a zillion catalogues. Nothing positive there.

Naturally, there wouldn't be any prints on it. The lab could work miracles with lasers and some chemicals, but the blood would have virtually obliterated any possible prints on the smooth surfaces. And the bone handle was too convoluted to provide a satisfactory print.

Holding the knife down with the eraser of a Ticonderoga Henry tested the edge of the blade with the ball of his thumb. Damn sharp. Even so, he had trouble visualizing the small knife blade being adequate for severing Trejo's head. But then he had trouble visualizing most of the murder weapons locked in the police property room being used in violent crimes. They were so passive: hammers, rocks, pieces of furniture. Somehow they failed to generate a vivid recreation of the crime. He was just not visually oriented. Definitely right brained. Or was it left? Maybe that was why he was slow on a case. Probably his German-Dutch heritage. He was a plodder, someone who meticulously assembled the bits and pieces, then mothered them like a goose with goslings, shifting them in a mental jigsaw puzzle until finally a picture emerged. But it was a painstaking process with few flashes of brilliance. He envied the guys with the quicksilver minds who could look at a knife like this and have the entire crime flash before their eyes, including a description of the killer, usually wrong. Fortunately, those kinds of people were as rare as World Series pennants in Dodger stadium.

He slid the knife back into the plastic bag and placed it in the desk drawer he reserved for data on the Trejo murder. Except for the knife and his note pad the drawer was empty. Also empty of ideas. He'd have to get the knife to the lab on Temple Street. Who knows, his luck might just change and they would get a print.

He took the note pad from the drawer and flipped it open. He never had any trouble deciphering his notes. His precise lettering could be read by anyone. Lots of data on Trejo himself and on Trans-America, but nothing on the killer except that he may or may not be the same man who'd been thrown out of Trejo's office. The woman said the stranger claimed the company owed him money. But there was no way of finding out when he'd worked for Trans-Am…or where. They had construction projects in several countries, including Trejo's native Ecuador. They must have hundreds of foreign workers on their payroll. It would take months to sort through company records. If he had a name a computer could run him down in seconds. But killers were too damn inconsiderate to leave their name lying around. Well, as the saying went: welcome each rebuff that turns life's roughness smooth.

He turned his thoughts to the matter of Trejo's severed head. Now that was different. It could have been severed for a number of reasons, the most logical being revenge. Cutting off the man's head could have been a further acting out of the killer's rage. And maybe he'd wanted to show it to another person as proof that his honor had been avenged. Would a paid killer need that kind of proof he'd done his job? No, all the proof he needed would be in the next day's newspaper. What about a warning to associates of Trejo? That smacked of organized crime, like the horse's head in Puzo's book.

Henry put his chin in his hand. How could he keep a positive outlook when everything was negative? He would need a hell of a lot more pieces to the puzzle before he could make a case. And the shrunken head? Probably a souvenir. But when was it purchased? And where?

He sat up sharply as a faint ray of light separated from the swirl of dark patterns in his mind. Hadn't he read somewhere recently that certain native tribes of Ecuador continued the practice of headhunting? And Trejo was from Ecuador. Maybe the killer was a headhunter. A native. From the jungles of Ecuador? Was that possible?

But if the killer was a headhunter, why had he abandoned the heads? And what would one of those savages be doing in Los Angeles? Could he fit into the urban environment without being seen? Extremely improbable. He would be about as inconspicuous as a clown in a nudist camp. So that left him exactly nowhere.

He put the note pad back in the drawer and closed it. He glanced at his old LeCoultre: 11:00 o'clock. Maybe Gene Wood had learned something by this time.

He got up and threaded his way around the steel desks in the big room, most of which were deserted, their occupants out on the streets badgering antagonists for information. Antagonists was right. He could remember when good citizens were willing, even anxious, to come forward with information. Now, with few exceptions, people were afraid of what might happen to them if they testified, or they were afraid of the endless time they would have to spend in court, and with good reason. Well, *c'est le guerre.* If the job was easy they wouldn't pay detectives such handsome salaries, less than many cities paid their street sweepers and bus drivers.

Henry took the elevator to the basement and Gene Wood's office where he walked in without knocking. The pathologist looked up from an X-ray, reproach in his eyes. When he saw that the intruder was Henry he relaxed.

"If you came here expecting me to do your job, forget it," he said. "If you came to invite me for coffee, I'll get my hat."

"You don't wear a hat." Henry smiled. "And if you did it'd have to be size three. Why haven't you got any clues for me?"

Woods led the way out the door. "Ah, I have. But it'll cost you."

Henry fell into step as they moved to the elevator. "Why is it that every time you have something for me it costs me?"

"You're lucky it's only coffee. If I had anything really good it'd be lunch."

Henry chuckled. "And if it's no good at all, I'm giving you the check."

At the corner of First Street they waited for the light and as he always did when the day wasn't too smoggy Henry gazed at the towering buildings of the L.A. skyline. He remembered the old skyline when the pointed top of the City Hall was the tallest building in the city. The soaring towers of the new city filled him with ambivalent feelings of pride and dread. The architects claimed their buildings were earthquake proof, but he'd hate to be eating in one of those expensive rooftop restaurants if they got hit with anything over 4.0 on the Richter scale. The building might survive, but he wouldn't. Besides, it wasn't right that the City Hall should be demeaned by surrounding the old girl with giants. She was supposed to be the proud guardian of L.A. But how could she be proud when half the people in the city could now look down on her pointy head?

He wasn't too fond of the new government buildings. The old stone monstrosities they'd torn down might have been crowded on the inside, but on the outside they had character. He promised himself that if he lived long enough to retire he would open some kind of an office in the old Bradbury building. Now there was a real building! With its huge central court, wrought iron balconies and hand-rubbed wooden balustrades, it was about the only building left with enough character to rate more than a passing glance from a tour bus.

The light changed and Henry was glad to hurry across the street and into the Copper Skillet where he could shut out images of ultra-modern buildings and the curb-to-curb flood of cars. They found an empty booth, to Henry's surprise. These days he expected to wait for everything. When you had to wait in line even to use a bank's ATM the city was definitely getting too damn crowded.

"Where is everybody?" he muttered. "Are we missing a spectacle someplace?"

Woods shook his head. "It's too late for coffee and too early for lunch."

Ramona, the plump Latina waitress, took their orders, grimacing when they said coffee *solomente.* "Your accents are lousy," she said.

"Okay, *muchacha*," Henry told her. "No *propina* for you."

"Big deal. Why should today be any different?" She poured coffee into their cups, slopping it into their saucers. "When you gonna make me a detective? I'd be great. I've got a sixth sense."

"If you had a sixth sense, you'd have slapped my face when you bent over to pour the coffee."

"How'd you like to work undercover?" Gene Woods asked. "I've got some great covers at my place."

Ramona shook her head. "You're too old. I'd kill you."

"Old!" Woods exploded. "I'm in my prime."

"I'd hate to have seen you before then." She turned to Henry. "When you gonna sign me up? All the young cops have already tried."

"Forget it, Ramona," Woods said. "He can't even take care of his wife."

Ramona knew Henry wasn't married and she winked. "No wonder. He's too busy takin' care of yours."

She laughed and moved away, swinging her ample hips. Henry watched her with pleasure. At least some things stayed the same. He took a sip of his coffee and reached for the sugar.

"What have you got?"

"Jesus," Woods said. "You should take a page from the Japanese. They at least go through the polite preliminaries before they hit you between the eyes."

"If I was Mr. Moto I wouldn't have to ask."

"Moto. You're really dating yourself."

Henry shrugged. "So I like old movies."

Woods sipped the oil-streaked coffee and made a face. "The victim was strangled. He was already dead when the head was severed."

"That must have been comforting. How long had he been dead?"

"Minutes. The deed was done immediately after death."

"Could you tell anything from the type of cuts?"

"He wasn't a surgeon, if that's what you mean."

"Was it done with that pocket knife?"

"That's what it looked like. If it had been sharper it would have been cleaner."

Henry remembered that the knife had been very sharp, but it was a far cry from a surgeon's scalpel. "I noticed the cuts seemed to be made low on the neck. Does that tell you anything?"

"Not me. Except that he probably wanted as much of the head as he could get."

Henry nodded. "That's what I thought, too. Makes sense if it was for revenge of some kind."

"Why else?"

"I sure as hell hope that was the reason."

Woods stared at him. "Why's that?"

"If the killer's had his revenge, that's the end of it. But if it was a madman, or some kind of a cult thing, he'll be hard to identify."

"If he doesn't do it again I doubt you'll ever catch him."

Henry looked away. Woods had touched a sore spot. A lot of people claimed that detectives weren't what they used to be. They were lazy or incompetent. The only killers they could catch were the obvious ones: the guy who took a baseball bat to his wife in a jealous rage, or the kid who got beat up on the Pacoima playground and went home and came back with a shotgun and blew the other boy's head off. But a real mystery requiring first class detective work usually brought them up empty. Charles Manson, the critics pointed out, was only caught because one of his family turned him in. The Skid Row Slasher was picked up for a stupid burglary and they accidentally found out he was the slasher. San Mineo's killer was turned in by his cell mate while he was in jail for another crime. The guy they called the Hillside Strangler had been picked up for crimes in another state.

"Yes," he admitted. "It's damn hard to run down killers when they don't have any connection with their victim."

"No connection? You think he picked Trejo's name out of a hat?"

"No. But the only connection is that Trans-Am or the Ecuadoran government owed him money, or he thought they did. But money for what? For work? And if so, was it here or Ecuador, or in some other part of the world? And when?"

"Assuming it was the same guy who broke into Trejo's office."

"That's right. It could have no connection with Trans-Am. Maybe it was a drug deal. Or a gambling debt. Trejo was known to like cock fights."

"Cock fighting is illegal."

"So is murder, but it's done every day." Henry took a long swallow of the tepid coffee. "All I've got to go on is that the killer may or may not have been crazy, he may or may not have been Latino, and he may or may not have been a headhunter."

"Headhunter. You mean like a cannibal?"

"Trejo was from Ecuador. They still have headhunters."

"And there was that trophy, which by the way was authentic."

"I thought it was. Headhunters. Jesus. Maybe I'd better get some help."

"I've been telling you for years you needed help."

"We might have a mad man here. I'll ask the Ecuadoran Consulate for information on the native tribes, the headhunters."

"Good idea. If it is a mad man, this might only be the beginning."

"That's what I'm afraid of."

CHAPTER 5

When Steve pulled his dusty Camaro into his driveway that evening Helen's Pinto was parked at the curb. He'd forgotten he had invited her over for dinner. After their first date he'd given her a key so she was probably inside. He hoped the sticking front door hadn't given her any trouble. Again, he wished he'd had time to make some repairs on the old house before she'd seen it.

One of the first things he'd done upon arriving in Los Angeles was draw from the bank what was left of his savings and make a down payment on a small home in Sunland north of Los Angeles, close to the foothills of the towering San Gabriel Mountains. Maybe it was his Apache heritage, but he never liked living in an apartment and he detested hotels and motels. The house was a little shabby with a lawn that looked as though it had last tasted water at the time of the Great Flood. But it was a home.

When he walked in he heard cupboard doors opening and closing. That was Helen. Instead of waiting to give him hell for being late, she was making dinner. Should he tell her about the blood on his clothes? How could he possibly explain? He'd better keep the whole thing to himself until he had some answers. Unless…he sucked in his breath. Suppose she'd seen the blood? He'd worked hard on the bathroom, but had he cleaned away all traces? And how could he explain it if he hadn't? But maybe she hadn't been in the bathroom and he was worried for nothing. He'd have to play it by ear. If he had to come up with an explanation the best thing would be the truth. It was all he had.

Helen's back was to him when he came into the kitchen and he stood for a moment watching her prepare dinner admiring the fluid grace of her movements. She was almost as tall as he, with wide shoulders and a narrow waist that flared into good hips. Her hair was a mass of ringlets. When she turned to reach for a plate Steve had a glimpse of her wide-spaced gray eyes under dark eyebrows.

Watching her putter around the kitchen gave him a sensation of contentment. He liked the warm joy of coming home to his woman. They belonged together, here, in his home. Maybe he should ask her to marry him. The idea amused him. He had never considered getting married. He'd always had too much fun catting around. Maybe he was getting old. Maybe instead of being a buck antelope who took every female he could during a perpetual rutting season he had turned into a mallard duck that preferred to settle down with one mate for life.

She gave a squeal, almost dropping a plate. "Steve! Don't do that."

"Do what?" He stepped to her and cupped her chin in his hand and kissed her, enjoying the warmth of her lips as they softened and responded. "Don't sneak up on me. You're going to give me a heart attack."

"Fat chance," he grinned. "You've got a heart like a stone."

"Louse." She aimed a playful kick at his shins which he sidestepped deftly.

He crossed to the stove and sniffed. "Smells good. What did you do? Send out?"

She moved to block his view. "After that crack yours is going to be a surprise."

Steve felt some of the tension ease. She couldn't have seen anything in the bathroom or she would not be so lighthearted. Even so, he had to be sure.

Keeping his voice casual, he said, "I'm going to wash up. Did you notice? I cleaned the bathroom this morning."

He was afraid she would see the anxiety in his eyes, so he turned his back to her. It seemed her answer would never come.

"It looked as messy as ever to me. What did you clean it with; old cement sacks?"

The last hold was released on his fear and he laughed. "Why not? If they're good enough for washing my face they're good enough for the tub."

In the bathroom he looked around. He'd done a pretty fair job. There were still a few signs of the horror of last night, but they wouldn't be evident to someone not looking for them. He turned on the faucets and washed his hands. The fear of discovery had ebbed, but the anxiety remained. Why couldn't he remember? Last night was lost in the vague memory of a throbbing headache that had filled his brain with too much pain for a night of boozing. Now he felt another one coming on. He bathed his face with water, trying to cool the heat that was building inside his head. It didn't help.

He opened the medicine cabinet and shook two aspirin out of the large bottle. Then he added a third. Lately two aspirin didn't help much. He'd have to buy more. The bottle was already two-thirds empty and he'd only had it a week. He hadn't realized he was taking so many. That couldn't be good for his stomach, or his liver, or what the hell ever else aspirin wasn't good for. But how could he cut down when the damned headache refused to go away? At its best, it was a throbbing ache. At its worst it burned through his brain like a blowtorch. He swallowed the three aspirin then added a fourth. He would rather risk every organ in his body than endure that kind of agony very long.

The anguish hadn't been helped by this morning's surprise. What the hell could have happened? Shit. He'd meant to buy a paper on the way home. There might have been something that would give him a clue. He stared at his reflection in the mirror unable to meet his own eyes. Did he really want to know? But if there was something how long could he avoid it? Worse. How long before it caught up with him?

"Did you read today's paper?" he called.

"Why? You in it?"

Steve leaned his forehead against the cold glass of the mirror. Was he in the paper? Dear God, he prayed not. He tried to keep his voice flat as he said, "I'm not famous. Just curious."

"About what?"

Steve was startled by the nearness of her reply and, turning, saw she was standing in the open doorway.

"Nothing special." He resumed washing his hands. "The way things are going we could be in a war."

"If you'd break down and subscribe to a paper you could keep up with the world."

Steve shook his head. "I never was much for reading."

"Well, you haven't missed much. That mess in the Middle East is all over the front pages."

"No juicy murders?"

He dared not look at her. Indians were supposed to be able to hide their emotions, but he felt as though his face was about as hard to read as the scoreboard at Dodger Stadium. Instead, he began lathering his face for shaving.

"I don't know. I only read the headlines. You expecting one?"

A chill made his hand tremble. Should he be expecting one? To conceal his interest, he chuckled.

"That bastard Gordo Sanchez. I almost killed him today. Someday somebody will." He pursed his foam-lathered lips at her, and she retreated to the kitchen.

He turned back to the mirror and ignored the lines of worry deepening between his eyes. He watched the safety razor cut a clean swath through the lather. When the stroke reached his neck, his hand began trembling so violently he had to stop. What the devil was going on? Did this morbid fascination with his throat have anything to do with the flash of memory of a man's body? Would there be anything about it in the paper? Somehow, he knew there would. And he didn't want to read it.

With an effort he resumed shaving. Hell, he wouldn't kill anybody. He'd been in plenty of fights, sure. But he'd never killed anybody. There had to be another reason for the blood. More likely he'd tried to help somebody who was injured. Yeah. That had to be it. He stared at his mirrored image as though it could provide answers. Could the loss of his memory be caused by the headaches? That had to be it. And when they went away he would be okay. If he was lucky he would never know what happened last night.

Sitting across from Helen at the small dining room table he picked at the T-bone steak. His appetite had almost vanished and he saw Helen glance at him with a frown. He wanted to drive away her fears with a few jokes, happy talk. But he couldn't until he set his mind at rest about last night. He did remembered picking Helen up at her place. They'd planned on going to a movie after dinner. Yes, that was right. And in the middle of dinner his headache had gotten so bad he'd begged off and taken her home. Then he'd come back here. Hadn't he?

"I want to apologize about last night." He watched her face, searching for any flicker that would tell him if she knew anything. "I hope I didn't drink too much."

"You only had a beer." She smiled mischievously. "Boy, have you

incomplete sentence

"I'll say. I offered to put you to bed, but you said your headache was killing you. That's a switch." She leaned forward to place her hand on his. "What is it? Something's really bugging you."

Steve liked the feel of her warm hand, but he didn't want her to feel the tremble so he pulled his hand away. "I guess I haven't really gotten over that Ecuador thing."

Helen left her hand extended across the table. "That was weeks ago. You've been out of the hospital more than a month."

Holding his smile was about as easy as walking on glass. "Yeah? Well, those Ecuador hospitals aren't the greatest."

"They must have been pretty good. You've got your quota of body parts."

There was a question in her voice. How much should he tell her? The questions would have to be answered sooner or later. Should he tell her everything? Did he dare? She might not be able to accept that he had been a headhunter. But if he asked her to marry him she would have to know. It wouldn't be fair if he didn't tell her. Maybe after they'd spent more time together. He didn't want her reacting like that idiot nurse in Quito

He said, quietly, "It wasn't that kind of an accident."

Helen gave up all pretense of humor. "Then what? You were gone for years; not a card or letter after the first few weeks. You just vanished. Then suddenly you show up here looking, well, different. And you have these headaches. You've got to tell me."

She cared about him a lot. Hell, she was in love with him. He was sure of it. She had a right to know. Beside, there was nothing to be ashamed of. It could have happened to anybody. What he didn't want to talk about were the blackouts. A strong man did not have blackouts, especially blackouts that lasted three years. But this was Helen. She would understand. "Okay." Deciding to tell her made him feel better. "You know I was working for Trans-Am on that road construction project in Ecuador."

"Yes."

"We got raided by Jivaros."

"By what?"

"Jivaros. Headhunters. The last thing I remember was getting hit on the head. When I woke up I was in a hospital in Quito with a bump on my head the size of a doorknob. Everybody else in the crew was killed."

"Why weren't you?"

"I think it was because they thought I was some kind of a shaman. Kind of a brujo, witch doctor. Because I could run the bulldozer."

"But that doesn't explain the three years."

Steve swallowed hard. "I know. When I woke up in the hospital it wasn't three weeks after the attack, it was three years."

"Years? Where were you?"

"That's just it. I don't know. Not for sure."

She stared at him waiting for him to explain. He would almost rather tell her he'd been living with another woman. She would be hurt, but she wouldn't be afraid. He would have to make her understand that what had happened wasn't his fault.

"They told me they picked me up after a Jivaro raid on some gold prospectors."

"You were a prospector? For three years?"

"No." He watched her for signs of revulsion. "It seems…I was a Jivaro."

She stiffened, her face set in lines of shock. "A headhunter?"

"That's the part I don't know." He couldn't stand the look in her eyes, and he pushed out of his chair. "At the hospital they figured I'd lived with the Jivaros those three years. I had to have been one of them."

"And you don't remember?"

"Not a thing." He walked to the dark fireplace and braced his hands on the mantel. "It's a total blank. Temporary amnesia they called it. It can happen from a blow on the head. Sometimes another blow'll snap you back. That's what happened to me."

Helen sat staring at her plate. "Those natives; what are they like?"

Steve laughed. In the hospital with time on his hands he'd done a lot of research on the native tribes. What he'd learned had astonished him.

"Complex as hell from what I could learn. The best jungle fighters in the world, because they're always at war with somebody."

"War? Who with?"

He turned to face her. "You've heard of blood feuds? Their entire lives from generation to generation are nothing but feuding. It's their religion."

"Religion?"

He groped for the words that would explain. "You see, what we call reality, this life, the things around us…well, to them this is the unreal. Their real world is one you can only see when you're under the influence of a hallucinogenic drug, and they've got a lot of them. They can be mild, like a drink they call *nateena*, or they can put you out of your skull. Everything bad that happens in what we call the real world is caused by an enemy spirit. There's no such thing as accidental death. Somebody dies from a snake bite, or a tree falls, he drowns, a fever…it was caused by an evil spirit sent by some shaman who'd been paid to do it. That means you've got an enemy and you've got to find out who and kill him before he wipes out your family. So you get your own shaman—it might even be the same guy—and you get him to give you some good spirits, and you go out and kill the guy who you think killed your family member. Then, so his ghost won't come back, you take his head, where his spirit lives. You've got to keep it long enough to perform three ceremonial 'soul-killing' dances, so the guy's spirit will be set loose and won't come after you. The whole thing might take weeks. That's why they shrink the head, make it into a *tsantsa*, so it'll be easier to carry and so it'll keep until after the final dance. Once the ceremonies are over the *tsantsa* isn't of any use so they throw it away or sell it."

Helen shuddered. "That's barbaric."

"Not to them. You've got to take the head or the guy's spirit will kill you."

Helen stood up and began clearing the table. "Do you think that during those three years you did something like that?"

Steve sank into his chair and stared at his hands. How many times in the last few weeks had he asked himself that same question? "I wish to God I knew."

"Do they kill other people?"

"They kill anybody they think is an enemy."

"And take their heads?"

"Not always. The Jivaros don't believe that white men have souls. But heads have been bought having red hair…some with blonde hair."

"Those headaches, do you suppose they're from the injury?"

"They didn't think so at the hospital. They took X-rays, all kinds of tests. The only thing is—" He stopped, wondering how much he should tell her about the blackouts.

"What is it?"

This was the part he dreaded. "Well, I have blackouts some times. They're short, but maybe I've just been drinking too much."

Helen bit her lips. "Maybe you'd better see a doctor here."

That was another fear he'd been trying to ignore. His fear of doctors was crazy, but he couldn't help it. The fear had been reinforced by his mother's death. She'd been in the care of a doctor and she'd died anyway. Cancer. If he had something that bad he would prefer not to know. Which was a stupid attitude. The sooner a serious illness was diagnosed the better the chances were that it could be cured. But he'd always healed up before without a doctor. All he needed was a little more time.

"Hell, I'll be okay. I've gotten over worse things than this."

Helen crossed to him and put her arms around his neck. "Of course, you will. Thank God it's over."

"Yeah," Steve said. But he thought about the blood on his clothes and he was glad she couldn't see his face. "I'm glad it is, too."

CHAPTER 6

During the night a Santa Ana wind swept in from the furnace of the Mojave Desert through the San Gabriels and down into the Los Angeles basin, pushing the smog out to sea where it hovered like a malignant veil until it could again smother the city. With the wind came the desert heat, sending the temperature rocketing a hundred degrees, and the Jivaro warrior stirred in his sleep. He twisted on the soaking sheets racked by nightmares of enemies trying to steal his soul.

Throwing aside the upper sheet and thin blanket he fought against the images that slashed through his sleep. There was no sense of dreaming, no subconscious awareness that this was an illusion. The Jivaro shaman sitting in the filth of the long jungle house pointing at him and drinking *nejimanche* beer laced with *nateema* was vivid. So, too, were the shaman's words as he told the warrior that an enemy was throwing evil darts at him. "Kill your enemy. Kill him before he kills you."

Squatting in front of the intense shaman barefoot and bare-chested with his hips wrapped in the customary cloth skirt the warrior was not surprised that an enemy was trying to kill him. The pain in his head was proof of that. The shaman was right; he must take his blowgun and find his enemy before it was too late. He searched the ground in rising panic, but he had no blowgun. The long tube he purchased from the Achuras had vanished, as had his pouch of darts smeared with ampi poison. He was defenseless against the powerful forces of his enemy. He had to make a new blowgun.

The warrior got out of bed, fighting the stultifying dry heat that was so different from the steam of the jungle, and walked outside to his machine where he picked up the length of plastic tubing and carried it into the place called a garage. At a cluttered workbench he made light with a switch on the wall.

Something was wrong. This was a strange material he held in his hand. Not wood. It was light, and white in color, and it already had a hole down the middle. The hole was larger than he would have liked, but it would have to do. His enemy was growing stronger and must be stopped.

The first thing to do was make the hole very smooth so that a dart could pass through it without snagging. Working rapidly he reamed out the inside of the hollow tube with sand on paper until it was velvet smooth. From a small block of balsa wood he fashioned a mouthpiece and fitted it to the end of the tube.

Now he had a blowgun; but what about darts? They should be made of slivers from the chonta palm. But there were no slivers. The palm trees outside of this place had needle-pointed pikes at the base of their fronds, but they were too weak to penetrate without buckling. No; he needed something strong.

He searched around the enclosure. Then he saw it: a wheel from a thing called a bicycle. The wires called 'spokes' would make good darts. He took the wheel to the workbench and used tools he found in a box to cut the spokes into six-inch lengths. Then he used the bench grinder to hone one end into a sharp point.

What to put on the other end? When a Jivaro wanted to shoot a dart, he took a tuft of wild kapok from a gourd and twisted it around the end of the dart. Inserted in the blowgun, the cotton material sealed the tube so that the full force of the hunter's breath could drive the dart out of the blowgun. But he had no kapok. What could he use? What were those things inside that glass? Corks. If they were the correct size they would be perfect.

He tried one of the small corks inside the blowgun. It was a shade small, but it would do. One by one he forced the corks over the blunt end of the steel darts. When he inserted one in the blowgun it fit snugly and he bared his teeth in satisfaction.

Raising the blowgun to his lips in a familiar gesture he selected for a target a round piece of metal called a hubcap that was hanging on the far wall. Without aiming, he fired. He was a big man with a huge lung capacity and the dart, moving too fast to be seen, streaked the length of the enclosure and, with a *thwack*, pierce the metal and buried half its length in a supporting two-by-four.

He visualized Jivaro warriors watching from the jungle and they nodded in approval. This was the best dart they had ever seen. The shaft of steel was stronger than chonta wood and even without a coating of ampi, such a dart could kill an enemy if he were hit in the right place. Yes, the blowgun was good, the other warriors would say. But what of the man? This white warrior was different. He was a stranger and while his courage had been proven on many hunts and during raids designed to help a friend kill an enemy, he had never hunted an enemy of his own. There was a way to prove his courage, just as the old ones had proven their courage: he could take his place on the Chullachaqui tower.

The warrior looked up at a small platform constructed fifty feet in the air on a cut-off tree trunk. He would have to do it, not only to prove his courage to himself, but to show the other warriors that he was not afraid of the spirit darts of his enemy nor the tangible darts of man. Quickly he scaled the tree trunk and pulled himself to a standing position. Looking down, he watched the Jivaro warriors pick up their blowguns and prepare their ampi-coated darts. He felt calm and strong climbing to the platform, but now the earth seemed far below. If a dart struck him it would weaken him enough to make him fall. He had seen that happen twice. Each time the man had frozen in fear and been struck by a dart. The image of their long fall and broken bodies was burned into his memory and, now, made his head ache with a sickening dread.

But that would not happen to him. None of the other warriors could fire a dart as fast as he, and none could move more quickly. Others had survived the Chullachaqui; he, too, could survive. If he didn't panic.

Watakateri, who was a *kakaram,* or 'powerful one' because he had killed many men, was to take the first shot. From his perch the white warrior saw Watakateri twist a tuft of kapok on the end of a poisoned dart and insert it in his blowgun. Almost before he could prepare himself Watakateri raised the blowgun to his mouth and fired. To his surprise he was able to see the dart coming up at him. Although it was moving as fast as the arrow from a powerful bow it seemed to move in slow motion, and also in slow motion he twisted aside just enough for the dart to pass so close he could feel the ripple of air on his bare skin. But the maneuver threw him off balance and he teetered on the platform while fear clutched his mind.

He was just regaining his balance when Wambia, the next warrior, fired at him. Again there was the feeling of slow motion, and this time he twisted away from the dart's deadly path without the convulsive effort that had almost cost him his footing before. When the next warrior fired he was poised, the fear under control. As long as he was prepared, his mind and body under control, they could not harm him. Time after time he watched the darts come up at him like evil spirits which he easily eluded.

But as the darts continued to come faster and faster he was forced to move with increasing speed, and it seemed that each time he evaded a dart, the evil spirit of his enemy came closer. He felt himself slip into frantic, uncoordinated movements, reeling away from a deadly sting. He was drenched with slimy sweat, teetering on the edge of the platform. Far below he dimly saw the last of the Jivaro warriors raise his blowgun and fire. It should have been easy to elude, except that he was almost frozen, his body demanding rest, unable to react. But the warrior was young and anxious and the dart thudded into the bottom of the platform where it quivered with a thin whine.

The shaman pointed up at him and shouted at the watching spirits that this was a brave warrior and was protected from the evil of El Diablo. Then he motioned for the white warrior to come down. Slowly he straightened, unable to believe that the ordeal was over. He'd won. Now he was truly a Jivaro. When he reached the ground he was exhausted. He staggered into the long house where he found his bed and collapsed. His last thoughts were that he must find his enemy and kill him and take his head. Only then would his head stop hurting, and he would once more roam the jungle in peace.

The alarm clock awakened Steve Kelly and he sat up, clinging to memories of another nightmare. His muscles were stiff and cramped. It was an effort to turn off the alarm and pull himself from the tangled sheets. Why should he be so tired after eight hours of sleep? It had to be the nightmares. And the headaches. They were draining him. Even now, his head throbbed. If he didn't get better soon he would have to find something stronger to take than aspirin. Willing his sore muscles into movement he took a step and his foot struck a length of plastic conduit lying on the floor. How the hell did that get in the house? He had left it in his car.

He picked up the plastic tube and was surprised that it was fitted

with a mouthpiece. What the hell for? Of course, a blowgun. A blowgun?
Here? Several steel blowgun darts in a leather pouch were lying on the
floor. How the hell did they get into his house? Had he brought them in?
Why couldn't he remember? Not another blackout!

He dropped the blowgun and the darts in a corner and walked into
the bathroom, afraid of what he might find. But the bathroom was clean.
He let his breath out slowly. Why had he expected to find blood?

CHAPTER 7

Henry Warner stood in LAX's Bradley Terminal and surveyed the passengers who had completed their customs' inspection and were filing past him. He hoped that Dr. Perez would recognize him from his description because he had no idea what the Doctor looked like. The conference had been arranged by the Ecuadoran consulate yesterday when he had asked them for an expert on native headhunters. It hadn't occurred to him that they would fly someone in at the expense of the LAPD, of course.

Now he stared in bewilderment at the hoard of people hurrying past, all discharged from the big Boeing 747. They seemed to be a total polyglot made up of Anglos, Latinos, and Asians wearing a variety of clothing styles ranging from grunge to business suits, all lugging boxes and bags. And lots of children. Only a handful of passengers were traveling alone. He concentrated on these, looking for someone with the uncertain expression of someone who expected to be met. If they missed connections he hoped the doctor would contact the consulate, otherwise they might never get together. Thank God he had stipulated that the consultant would have to speak English. He could at least have him paged.

He smiled in quiet chagrin. Dummy. He could have him paged in Spanish. The people at the airline's ticket counter were bilingual.

The last of the passengers filed through the gate, when someone said, "Lieutenant Warner?"

The vibrant voice held a trace of accent and Henry turned wearing his best welcome smile. The smile became fixed and his outstretched hand froze. The voice belonged to a woman who could have stepped straight out of a brochure of Spain. She was not tall, although in her high-heels her eyes were almost level with his. But she was slender so she seemed tall. She was wearing a navy-blue skirt and a white blouse that looked as though it was made of satin. Her jacket of black and white checks was wide of shoulder, buttoned at her small waist, and flared over her hips. She had a maroon and gold scarf tied loosely around her neck European style. Its colors accentuated the pale bronze of her clear skin. Her blue-black hair was pulled back and fastened in a coil at the nape of her neck so that her small, diamond earrings caught the light. But her eyes were magnificent: large and dark with long lashes, highlighted by thick, natural eyebrows. And her lips; full, sensuous, parted in a smile that had the stunning power of an electric shock.

"You have to be Lt. Warner," she said. "Only a detective would be so…analytical."

Henry felt his face grow warm. "Yes." To his irritation his voice had reverted to the high tenor of a teenager. "But are you Dr. Perez?"

"I am."

"Doctor I. Perez?"

"Irene. Yes."

"Oh, Irene. Of course." Henry mentally shook himself. She was going to think he was a mental case. His face broke into a smile to match hers. He dropped his voice to a baritone. "My apologies. It's just that I was expecting a man. I mean, the consulate didn't tell me that Dr. Perez was a woman."

"Then I should apologize. They should have made it clear in the communication."

"Well, I'm certainly glad you're here." He reached for the two bags she was carrying. "I'll have the rest of your baggage picked up."

She gestured. "This is total. They told me I would only be here a few days."

Henry was on the edge of being dumbfounded. A woman who dressed with such impeccable taste would usually be traveling with a ton of luggage. She had to be as efficient as she was beautiful. What was it she'd said? A few days? Maybe not. He picked up the bags and led the way through the crowed terminal.

"I hope you had a pleasant journey."

"Oh, yes. I enjoy traveling."

"Did the consulate explain what we're looking for?"

"Not much. I hope you will forgive me, but it has been a long time since I have used my English."

Henry enjoyed hearing her sound the unfamiliar syllables. "Nothing to forgive." He put on his most charming grin. "Your grammar is better than mine. For what that's worth."

"At least we seem able to communicate."

She had a good sense of humor. He was grateful for that. Some philosopher had said that you could never trust anyone who had no sense of humor. Henry took a gamble on impressing her. "You probably went to school in the States. My guess would be California. USC."

She made a sound of surprise. "Yes. I got my PhD there. Did they tell you?"

"No. They just told me that Dr. I. Perez would be coming in on that flight."

She glanced at him, her eyes sparkling. "Then you really are a detective. You learned all that from my voice?"

"A lucky guess," Henry admitted. "I couldn't believe you could speak English so well without living in an English-speaking country. That meant a university. Your elocution sounds more American than British. Ecuador is on the west coast of South America so it probably meant a west coast university. California was a logical choice. Presumably your family had money. Which means a privately endowed university. USC has a renowned anthropology department and since you are an anthropologist—or the consulate wouldn't have sent you. I put it together with your maroon and gold scarf with the little USC in the corner and made a brilliant deduction."

She laughed and Henry thought he had never heard such a lovely sound. "You are a very good detective. I am surprised you have not caught the criminal you are after."

The way she said words ending in 'ed' delighted Henry because she pronounced both letters the way it was done in Shakespeare's plays.

"The trouble is we haven't been able to get a handle on this guy."

"Get a handle?"

"I mean, identify him psychologically."

"I understand. But I don't see in which manner I can be of assistance."

"How much did the consulate tell you about the death of *Señor* Trejo?"

"Only that he was from Ecuador and you need the assistance of someone familiar with the natives of the Montaña. Although I do not understand the connection."

"His head was severed from the body. When we found it there was a shrunken human head next to it. Like the headhunters take. That's why we asked for an expert." He glanced at her. "I certainly didn't expect someone like you."

"You think a woman could not be an expert on the headhunters of the Montaña. Verdad?"

"Well, yes. You don't seem like the rugged, outdoor type. And, I know that in many Latin countries a woman's place is still considered to be in the, uh, kitchen." Jesus. He'd almost said 'in the bedroom'.

Her back stiffened. "That is true. And it is also the way many men feel about women here in your country."

"Not I," Henry said. He could hardly tell her that he had been in the forefront of the movement to increase the number of women on the Force and to advance them through the ranks to detective grade. Such an admission coming now would sound as though he was trying to justify his statement. "In any event, I asked for an expert. There's no reason why a female shouldn't be as good an anthropologist as a man." He saw that most of the tension had gone out of her shoulders. "If you can take the easy life."

She smiled. "Forgive me. I sometimes forget that Americans...let us say that in my country it can be difficult for a woman to be accepted in a man's field. Perhaps I am too sensitive."

"No, I'm just a clod."

"A clod? What is that?"

"An insensitive stupido."

Again he experienced the pleasure when she laughed. They had reached the busy terminal street and Henry led the way into the public garage where he had parked his two-year-old Saturn.

As he held the door for Dr. Perez, she said, "It always surprises me, the police here."

"Surprises you? Why is that?"

She waited until he had put her bags in the trunk and had climbed in behind the wheel. "In my country the police would have parked in the 'No Parking' area in front of the terminal. After all, they are the polica."

"I might have done that if this were a company car. But if I get a ticket in this one I have to pay for it."

"Your ways may not be good for the police, but they are better for the people. I like that."

He became aware of her perfume. It was a faint memory of spring flowers. He wondered if she was married. He should have asked the consulate. That was a stupid thought. He could hardly have stipulated that should the consultant turned out to be female and with a voice that would heat an igloo she would have to be single. Anyone so attractive would probably be married. Except that she wasn't wearing a wedding ring. That thought was so pleasant that he savored it as he drove out of the parking area.

"You must be tired," he said. "I've booked you into the Bonaventure Hotel downtown. I think you'll like it. And it's close to the office."

She leaned back against the headrest. "I am a little. I will feel it more in a day or two. And perhaps by then my work will be finished."

"I hope so," Henry answered.

The odds were that if they didn't catch this nut soon they never would; unless he struck again. In any event, this might be a good time to bring her up to date so she could be thinking about it. He was a firm believer in the incubation of ideas. Bring all the information together, then let the subconscious do its job.

"Except for the business with the heads we don't have much to go on. Trejo had a lot of enemies, but we haven't been able to isolate any one of them who could have done this. We were hoping that you could tell us if it might have been done by a native."

"A native of the Montaña region?" She half turned to him, light and shadow playing across her face as the moved along Century Boulevard. "Here? In the city?"

"Trejo was from Ecuador. He could have an enemy from there."

She slowly shook her head. "It could not be a Jivaro—"

"A what?"

"A Jivaro. One of the headhunting tribes. But a native would not know how to survive in a large city. Out of the jungle they are children."

"Well, whoever killed Trejo knew something about them. That's why we need your help. We don't know a darn thing about how these people think or how they select their victims…nothing."

Irene Perez stared out the window as they made the freeway entrance and headed north toward the Santa Monica interchange. When he merged with the heavy flow of speeding traffic he saw her tense and her right hand moved to grip the door's armrest.

"Been a while since you've seen traffic like this, I'll bet," he said.

"Never. When I left here it was nothing like this."

Henry wondered when that had been. He could not remember when the traffic on the San Diego and the Santa Monica freeways hadn't been a solid crush of cars going both directions. "Don't worry about it." He chuckled to reassure her, but her right hand maintained its grip on the armrest while her left held her purse as thought she was prepared for trouble. "What makes you think he couldn't be a native?" he asked, to get her mind off the traffic.

She tore her eyes away from the traffic to look at him. "It is very complex. But this person you seek; he could not be a true native. They are far too primitive. Perhaps someone who lived with the Jivaros?"

"Seems more logical." Henry remembered the description Trejo's secretary had given them. "How about a construction worker?"

"Yes, yes. We have construction workmen come to Ecuador for road building, for the oil fields. If they spent time with the natives they could learn their customs."

"But why adopt them? And why use them here?"

She was again staring out the window at the cars rushing along the Santa Monica freeway, but she was more relaxed. "I cannot believe a sane person would take a human head."

"I'll buy that," Henry agreed. "But what I'd like to know is: do these Jivaros kill indiscriminately, or are they selective?"

Irene Perez placed her fingers together and held them up to her lips and Henry felt a surge of satisfaction. She was beginning to trust his driving. "The Jivaros never kill at random. Always there is a reason. But you must realize their reasons are not our reasons. You see, if I can put this simply, the native of the Montaña believes that he has more than one soul or *wakani*. The most important of these is the *arutam*, which is acquired during a vision. While he has it the *arutam* makes a person immune to death."

"That is important," Henry said wryly.

She caught his inflection and frowned. "A Jivaro only attacks when he believes that his victim has lost his soul or its power has declined. And each time he kills his own soul becomes stronger. A very great killer who has acquired many *arutam* souls is called a *kakaram*, the 'powerful one'. A *kakaram* is considered so invulnerable to death that no one even attempts to kill him."

"A regular killing machine."

"In a sense, yes."

Henry allowed the information to penetrate. It was difficult to accept that there were people who could believe such nonsense. Well, maybe not so difficult. When your spiritual leader—shaman, priest, rabbi, or mullah—tells you that something is the will of God it is difficult to contradict him. Who knows? He might be right.

"But what does that have to do with headhunting?"

"A native's other soul is the *muisak*. Its only purpose is to avenge the death of the person killed. That's why it comes into existence when a person is killed, provided he had an *arutam* soul in the first place. This rules out children and usually women, which is why they are seldom killed."

"Seldom?"

"Some women are thought to have acquired *arutam* souls. But they are rare."

"And no great honor, I would think."

"On the contrary." She was not smiling. "It is a great honor. It means the woman must be a very great person."

"So it's the avenging soul that is feared?"

"Yes. When a man is killed the *muisak wakani* is trapped in the head. So to carry it back to the killer's house he preserves the head, he makes it into a *tsantsa*."

"Shrinks it? But why?"

"Because later, using the *tsantsa*, he performs as many as three *hanlsamata* soul-killing dances. This expels the *muisak* and sends it back to its place of origin."

"I see. That's why they shrink the head, for preservation. So, what happens to the head when they're finished with this dance?"

"It has no value. Its spirit had been exorcised, so the head is thrown away. Lately they are sold because some people will buy them, although I don't know why."

"Some people will buy anything. But they won't sell it before the ceremony?"

"Never. It would be dangerous to even touch the head before the ceremony. It would be very bad."

"I hope the one we found was used. I'd hate to have its owner after me."

"Was the head...did it have dark skin?"

"Yes. Almost black. I thought it was because it was old."

"Not necessarily. When the *tsantsa* is made the skin is darkened to keep the spirit inside from seeing out."

"Makes sense. I wouldn't want it staring at me."

Irene Perez still did not smile. "I've lived with the Jivaros. They are a wonderful people...if they don't think you're an enemy."

As he had so many times Henry again wondered what caused a religion to take strange turns. This religion of the Jivaros evolved over hundreds of years, bit by bit adding to its taboos and dogma. In this case, its customs were bizarre and, worse, they were deadly.

"How does the Jivaro choose his victim?"

"He doesn't always chose them. He will kill in self-defense if it is necessary. But usually it's someone he thinks is trying to kill him. Perhaps someone who has hired a shaman to attempt to kill him by throwing darts at him."

Henry glanced at her in surprise. "Darts? Blowgun darts?"

"No, no. These are called *tsentsaks*, spirit darts, evil spirits. The shaman carries a supply inside his stomach. When he is hired he regurgitates a *tsentsak* and hurls it. The victim never knows when this is happening. But if the shaman throws it hard enough, so it passes all the way through the victim's body, he always died within a few days."

Henry shook his head. "Even if he doesn't know about it?"

"That's what makes it so peculiar. If it was psychological the victim would have to be aware that he was the target."

"You mean like pointing the bone in the Aborigine culture?"

"Yes. Except that with the Australian Aborigine the victim is always aware the spell is being directed at him. His own mind often causes his death."

"But a Jivaro doesn't know when a shaman has thrown an evil dart into him? So it couldn't be a...self-fulfilling prophesy."

"That's right. He doesn't know, but the strange thing is always he becomes sick. And if another shaman is not called in to suck out the evil spirit, he dies."

Henry shivered. "Weird."

"Not to them. You see, this world around us that we call reality is not as real to a Jivaro as the supernatural. What we call the supernatural is their reality. The spirits that inhabit the supernatural world are as real, perhaps more real, than the people he sees. He cannot see the spirit people, but they are all around him. Every event that occurs is a result of spirits in this other world. If he is hurt, or becomes sick it is because of an evil spirit."

"What about good spirits? Don't they help him?"

She smiled "You're thinking like a Christian. The Jivaros only have evil spirits. The good things are taken for granted. That is the normal, the way things are supposed to be. They do not need to 'happen.' It is only the bad that is abnormal, so it has to be made to happen. The shaman is the inter…how do you say…intermediary between the living and the dead." She glanced at Henry. "Is this helping?"

"I should be taking notes. I'll never remember all this."

Perez looked at the skyline of tall buildings. "What is that? We are not downtown?"

"No. That's Century City. Used to be the back lot of Twentieth Century Fox. Now it's a city in itself."

"I remember when they started," she said. "I had no idea it would be so big."

"The whole city has burgeoned. You won't recognize downtown."

"Then, in all of this, how do you expect to find one man?"

"It won't be easy." It occurred to Henry that this might be his opening. "I think we should continue our discussion, perhaps at dinner tonight. I mean, if you don't have plans."

"I had thought about looking up some old friends," she said. "But it would seem more important that we find this person who killed *Señor* Trejo, don't you think?"

"Oh, yes. Who knows what horrible things he might be planning? I'll pick you up at the hotel at seven?"

"Oh, yes. I forgot how early you go to dinner in the States. But, could we make it eight?"

As far as Henry was concerned, she could make it 4:30 on a Sunday morning on the planet Mars. He would be there. "Fine, Doctor. Eight it is."

"Oh, and one more thing. Please call me Irene."

"Okay. My name is Henry."

"Henry Warner." Henry liked the way she made his name sound, as though it was important to her. "I like that. You must tell me about your family."

"Tonight. I'll tell you everything." For the first time in his life he hoped he wouldn't find the solution to a case too quickly. He wanted this one to take a little time.

CHAPTER 8

Steve Kelly remembered little of his work. He had gone through the day in a daze, working the controls of the backhoe by instinct, fighting to grasp faint images of jungles and half-naked hunters that hovered on the edge of his memory. He fought to bring them into focus, but they remained tantalizingly vague until stabs of pain from another headache drove the elusive shadows into oblivion.

The other men saw the look in his eyes and stayed away from him. If he was high on something they didn't want to be around him. It wasn't much of a sacrifice. Steve had the reputation of being a loner, moving to the beat of his own solitary drum. They accepted it as normal behavior for an Apache. Hell, Indians could live their entire lives alone on the top of a mountain and think they were being crowded. If the big Indian wanted to be antisocial who gave a rat's ass?

Only Gordo Sanchez felt inclined to intrude on Steve's tortured thoughts. "Hey, slick," he shouted from the cab of his truck. "You got any more dough? Go ahead and lay another one on my rig."

He laughed and the ugly sound cut through the fog in Steve's mind. His enemy was taunting him! Steve's lips pulled back into a snarl, and he swung the manta-head of the backhoe in a vicious arc with the row of blunt teeth pointed at the windshield of Sanchez's battered truck. Sanchez yelped and dove to the floorboards and Steve stopped the backhoe's bucket inches from the windshield.

Sanchez looked up past the dirt-encrusted steel teeth into the depths of the bucket, which loomed like the gaping jaws of a Tyrannosaurus Rex. He became aware of the men laughing at him and his face changed from pasty gray to dull red. He reached for the door handle and Steve dropped the full weight of the bucket on the hood of Sanchez's truck with a heavy crunch that shook the big rig. Sanchez cursed and slammed open the door of the cab and jumped to the ground his face twisted in fury.

By the time he charged around the rear of the backhoe Steve had also jumped to the ground. The came together like two big horn sheep, their heads lowered, their bodies crashing together with a resounding thud. Sanchez's weight drove Steve back and the big Mexican wrapped both arms around him. Sanchez got one of his wrists locked in the other in the small of Steve's back and his muscles bulged in his huge arms, his foul breath clogging Steve's nostrils.

The pain on his back and ribs from Sanchez's bear hug increased the burning fury that flamed through Steve's brain, and he flailed with all the strength of his body. Sanchez might as well have tried to hold a panther. With a cry Steve smashed his head into Sanchez's chin and twisted from the powerful grip, smashing his elbow into the side of Sanchez's neck.

Sanchez fell back shaking his head, then he ripped at Steve with fists like sledge-hammers, and Steve was not looking at a Mexican construction worker; he was fighting for his life against a hated Acuna warrior. The enemy wanted his soul!

With a scream of rage he brushed aside the pounding fists and used his feet and hands to trip the Acuna. With a snarl he smashed both knees into the Acuna's chest and took his thick neck in his two hands and squeezed, feeling his fingers and thumbs sink into the flesh. The Acuna buckled and threshed wildly, clawing at his hands. But his hands were locked like the talons of a bird on a fish and he refused to let go no matter how hard the enemy warrior battered and clawed. Then other hands grabbed him, prying him away.

"Steve! For Christ's sake. You're killing him. Let go!"

Dimly he became aware of voices and he stopped fighting the hands, bewildered. Yes. He was Steve. Steve Kelly. And they were pulling him away from Gordo Sanchez who was sucking in air in massive wheezing gulps. He'd almost killed Sanchez. As much as the bastard deserved to die he didn't want that.

He straightened, and said, "I'm okay."

The men let go of him. When he walked away they moved aside. Nobody wanted to be in his path, not when his eyes were still fixed on some image that only he could see. And the image was of an enemy warrior. It was an image that Steve Kelly did not understand, but one that frightened him more than Gordo Sanchez ever would.

That evening when he arrived at Helen's 2nd floor apartment in La Crescenta he was still trying to pierce the veil that obscured the image.

Ordinarily he didn't like apartments, but this one was different. Helen had a flair for decorating. She had used wooden panels of knotty pine and pine furniture to create the illusion of a mountain cabin. The effect was enhanced by the scent from tall pines on a hillside behind the apartment building. Three aspirin had made his headache abate to an imperceptible throbbing, and he relaxed in a deep chair and let the scent wash over him while he listened to Helen as she prepared dinner in the open kitchen area.

The smell of the pines reminded him of the San Carlos Reservation and memories of his childhood drove away the faint image of the awful warrior. The happiest times of his life had been spent roaming the wild back trails of the huge Arizona reservation. He had always planned on returning someday when he could afford to build a good house. But there were few members left of his family; none he'd cared to keep in touch with. Still, the reservation was a place of peace, a good place to spend the mellow years. He would build a cabin up in the hills somewhere back above the Salt River. Helen would like it there, so wild and free. He was estimating how many years it would take him to save the money when Helen called him to dinner with the soft pressure of her lips on his closed eyelids.

"Come and eat," she said. "Then I'll rub some warm oil on your back and chest."

"Okay," Steve said with a smile. "Then I'll do the same for you."

She returned the smile. "It's only fair."

Helen was an excellent cook and Steve usually stuffed himself to the point of embarrassment. But he didn't have much of an appetite. It had to be because he hadn't fully recovered from three years of eating what the hell ever those stupid Jivaros ate. The way he'd been feeling lately it was going to take a damn long time. Still, his body needed the nourishment; also he didn't want Helen to worry, so he ate more than he wanted. He also tried to conceal the dull headache, but she caught him massaging his temples. Her clear forehead wrinkled in a worried frown.

"Steve," she said. "I'm really worried about those headaches. You should see a doctor."

Steve stared at his plate, toying with his knife and fork. "I don't like doctors much. My people don't trust them. Besides," he worked up a smile, "I'll be okay. I always heal up."

"Up to now. There's always the last time, the one that doesn't heal." She came around the table and put her hands on his shoulders. "It could be serious."

"I guess you're right." Her insistence only sharpened his anxiety that increased each time the throbbing behind his temples became worse. "The doctor in Quito gave me the name of a doctor here. He said I should call him if I started feeling bad."

She took a chair and faced him. "You've got to do it. You're not getting any better."

He looked up and saw that she was studying him, her eyes misty. The realization that she cared so deeply startled him. He desperately wanted the headaches to be temporary. They had to be. Hell, he'd never been sick a day in his life except for that time when they'd taken his tonsils out. And if they'd left him alone he would have been all right then, too. But it was going to be difficult to convince Helen.

"I could make a trip to the reservation," he said. "I know an old witch doctor who could cure a centipede with athlete's foot."

Helen realized that he was trying to reassure her. "You're only half Apache. You'll have to see an Irish priest for the other half."

"Jesus," Steve smiled. "A witch doctor and a priest. That's probably what's wrong with me. My poor soul doesn't know whether to go to heaven or to the happy hunting ground."

But Helen was too concerned to keep in the mood. "I still think you should—"

Steve put down his fork. "Look. Could we just drop this? I'm not going to any damn hospital."

Helen stared at him a moment. She used both hands to sweep her long hair back from her face as though to concede to a change of mood. "Why is it you grew up on the reservation? Your father wasn't Apache."

Despite the pain in his head, he smiled. He should have known that when Helen got her mind set on his health she would dog it to death. "My father worked for the railroad, a gandy-dancer."

"A what?"

"Gandy-dancer. Track repair man. When I was born they were living in Phoenix. I was only six when my father was killed in an accident. My mother went back to her people on the San Carlos. She had my dad's pension and we lived on that 'til she died. When that happened I just cut out."

"If you went back you could probably get in a government hospital."

A sharp burst of anger flared so hard that it blotted out the throbbing pain. He pushed back from the table so abruptly he toppled the chair. "Goddamn it! Stop trying to put me in a hospital! I told you, I ain't sick!"

Helen stared at him, her face ashen. "I'm not trying to make you do anything. It's just that those headaches might be serious and—"

"For Christ's sake!" he snarled. "Get off my back!"

He grabbed his jacket and stormed out, yanking the door shut behind him. He got in his car and screamed out of the parking lot onto the quiet street. He knew Helen was only trying to help him. But damn it! Why the hell couldn't she let him make up his own mind? Why couldn't they all leave him alone? That son-of-a-bitch Gordo Sanchez. It had started with him. He'd been okay when he got back on the job until that bastard started riding him. Then the headaches had gotten worse. As long as Sanchez was around they'd never stop. What was it the shaman had said? You must kill your enemies or they will send evil spirits into your head. Weren't the headaches proof that Sanchez was sending darts into his brain? Yes. It had to be him. And it would only end when his enemy was dead and he had performed the *hanlsamata*, soul-killing dance.

But how was he to kill Sanchez? His enemy would be in his house with his wives and relatives, and his only weapon was the blowgun he had made. A naked dart, even a formidable dart with a six-inch steel shaft, could not kill unless it was driven directly into his enemy's brain. Even a shot into the heart might not kill; the steel shaft was too thin. He would have to make some strong ampi poison mixed with snake venom and put it on the darts. Then a hit anywhere on the body would be fatal. He had seen three hundred pound peccaries brought down with a blowgun dart smeared with a mixture of ampi and venom from a Fer-de-lance or a Bushmaster. And Sanchez weighed a lot less than a wild boar.

But where would he get ampi? Even if he could locate a Chando vine and get some of its sap the ampi would have to be mixed with snake venom. Then a thought exploded through the pain: there were snakes in a place called a zoo. They probably had many that were poisonous. The venom of a Cobra or a Krait or a Pit Viper, any of them would do. All he had to do was find them.

Where was this zoo? Griffith Park. Yes, that was right. Just off the Golden State freeway. Not far. How late was it open? It was already past the time called nine. They wouldn't keep it open this late. And if they did, he could wait. They would have guards. But they would also have trees and bushes, and in the jungle, no one could see a Jivaro warrior if he didn't want to be seen.

The moon was up when he turned off the Ventura Freeway onto Zoo Drive. Along Crystal Springs Drive near the zoo machines were parked with groping couples inside. No one paid any attention when he pulled off into a pool of darkness and got out of his machine. He breathed deeply of air spiced with the odor of pepper trees. He tore away the restrictive cloth of his shirt. Now he was a warrior! He wished he had some of the red paint from urucu berries to put on his face. Then his enemies would be frightened to look upon him. But that would have to come later when he had killed his enemy, the man called Sanchez.

Moving silently he circled west through chaparral and manzanita at the edge of a golf course until he picked up the scent of animals. He turned to approach from the south, far from the main entrance. There was a chain-link fence around the periphery, but he went over it like a shadow. The paths throughout the zoo grounds were lined with shrubs and he moved rapidly, keeping to shadows made dark by the moonlight. He passed enclaves containing deer and antelope and exotic game from Africa, India, and South America. When he silently trotted past the cages of lions, tigers, cheetas, and cougars, the big cats paced restlessly, shattering the quietness with rumbling growls.

A guard came from a side path to investigate and the Jivaro melted into the darkness, circling the man who stood staring at the restive cats with a puzzled frown. When he found the reptile house there was another guard patrolling outside, and the Jivaro vanished into the bushes until the guard passed.

Inside, dim lights illuminated the aisles and many of the glass-fronted cages. The Jivaro drifted down the aisle like smoke, peering into the cages, searching for the familiar flashing colors of a Coral snake or the black-edged diamond markings and yellow chin of the Fer-de-lance. Behind the glass of one cage he recognized the black, slender body of a large Bushmaster but he passed it by. A Bushmasters would have the venom he wanted, but they were too aggressive. Virtually all snakes would avoid a fight, usually attacking a man only if they were threatened, or thought they were. But not the Bushmaster. It was one of the few snakes, perhaps the only snake that had been known to stalk a man and kill him. No, he wanted venom. But he also wanted to survive.

The next cage held an African Black Mamba. It raised its flat head when it saw the Jivaro and flicked the air with its tongue, feeling for telltale vibrations. This was the one. The Jivaro was unfamiliar with the species but he did know the important point: the Black Mamba had larger poison glands than any other snake. A big Mamba such as this one probably contained enough venom to kill several men.

Now he had to find something he could use to break the glass and kill the snake.

Outside the reptile house, he was reaching for one of the boulders used to line the paths when he saw a heavy metal rod with a small U in one end and he recognized it as the rod used to turn the lawn sprinklers on and off. It would be perfect, not only for breaking the glass but for pinning down the snake until he could kill it.

He checked the path before he went back inside. No guards were in sight.

When he broke the thick glass of the cage with the heavy handle of the rod, the frightened snake retreated to the far end as he had expected, and moved into a defensive coil, its head up and weaving slightly, its yellow eyes open wide and its black tongue darting frantically.

He slowly swung the U shaped end of the rod in front of the snake. But it refused to strike, its sensitive temperature sensors telling it that the rod was not the enemy.

The Jivaro smiled. Smart snake. Never waste energy on a false target. He shifted the rod to his right hand and slowly moved his left hand toward the snake's head. When it struck he yanked his hand aside and, moving with the same blinding speed, pinned the outstretched head down with the U in the rod.

Holding the snake firmly pinned, he picked up a shard of glass and slashed off the head. He released the rod and while the snake's thick body beat at the cage walls in a convulsive dance of death, he picked up the head, carefully avoiding the fangs which, even now, would kill him if they got the chance.

Moving fast, he left the building and vanished into the shadows of the trees just as two guards strode down the path. They were trying to decide if they had really heard the sound of breaking glass in the reptile house and, if they had, which one was going to go inside to see if one of the creatures had somehow managed to escape.

Near his machine, the Jivaro found an empty plastic butter container in a picnic trash basket. He cleaned it with leaves, then milked the poison from the head of the Mamba into the container. They had been right about the big snake. Its huge poison glands produced more venom than he had ever seen.

When he finished, he threw the snake's head into the bushes. He carefully fitted the lid on the container of milky fluid and put it in the machine, wedging it so it would not turn over. The venom would add a deadly potency to the darts. But he still had to have ampi. Where could he get it? The Jivaros always purchased the poison from the Achuara who made it from the sap of a Chando vine. A shaman had once shown him how they made it, and if he could only locate one of the vines, he knew he could recall the way it was done. But where? It would have to be a place where there were trees from many lands just as the zoo had animals from many lands.

Of course. A botanical garden. He dimly remembered there was such a place nearby. But where? Off the Foothill Freeway. Arcadia. He had passed a sign many times on his way to Santa Anita Racetrack. There was a name. Spanish? It meant 'to rest'. Descanso. That was it. Descanso Gardens.

He was driving by instinct, his hands and feet and a part of his mind going through the mechanics conditioned into his reflexes by years of practice. But his mind was focused on an image of jungle trails and a shaman who moved ahead of him like a specter, searching for the illusive Chando vine. And when he found it, using his machete to chop the thick creeper into short lengths, which they carried back to the shaman's house.

He turned off the freeway at Baldwin Avenue and almost immediately saw the sign. Descanso Gardens, the LA County Arboretum.

He parked the machine in heavy darkness outside the grounds and got out, his nostrils filled with the cloying scent of gardenias and jasmine.

He scaled the fence and dropped silently inside the grounds. He paused and peered at the profusion of trees and plants, starkly quiet in the moonlight. How would he find the Chando vine in this miniature jungle? Would he recognize the vine if he saw it? Yes. He would know it just as he knew how to use the blowgun.

He trotted slowly along a pathway, scanning the trees and bushes for the telltale leaves of the Chando vine. Then he discovered that each tree was designated with a small plaque near its base, but it was too dark to read the printing. He would have to rely on his memory.

He wondered if there would be guards here. It seemed likely and he increased his pace, moving with silent speed, pausing only to check an occasional thick, twisting vine. Many looked so much like the Chondo that he had to examine them closely, but none had the familiar smooth bark and waxy leaves.

Near the center of the Gardens he encountered the buildings of a visitor's center. Through the glass of the entrance he saw a black man sitting at a desk. The guard? But why wasn't he out on patrol?

He learned the answer while working his way through a tangle of strangely shaped trees near the north fence. He noticed the shadowy form of a huge bird roosting in the low branches of a tree. What was it? A turkey? Unlikely. The bird shifted uneasily and the Jivaro saw its head. A peacock. No wonder the guard did not find it necessary to patrol. Peacocks and peahens were, perhaps, the best watchers in the world, better even than dogs. He would have to move with extreme care.

It took him several minutes to circle the tree where the birds were nesting, watching carefully for others. In a way it was fortunate the birds had forced him to make the detour because just off the central path he found a Chando vine, its thick stock looping around the trunk and branches of a tall Jacaranda tree.

But how could he cut the lengths he needed? The vine was far too thick and too strong to be torn apart with his bare hands. He reached in his pocket for his small knife, then remembered that it had disappeared.

He would have to find a cutting tool of some kind. There had to be a maintenance tool shed of some sort nearby, maybe near the building where the guard was.

Moving with care, he returned to the buildings where he located a storage shed. Its door was secured by a large padlock through a hasp. He took the lock in both hands and cautiously twisted until the screws holding the hasp tore loose from the wood with a soft popping sound.

Quickly he opened the door and stepped into the darkness, pulling the door shut behind him. He felt for a thing on the wall that made light and when he found it, snapped on the light. The room was cluttered with ropes, saws, ladders and various types of digging tools. But his eyes were drawn to a pruning machete hanging from a nail on the wall. When he lifted it down, the machete had a familiar feel. Yes, he was very familiar with machetes.

Returning to the Chando vine, he paused. There was no way to avoid disturbing the roosting birds when he chopped the vine loose from the tree. And the birds would bring the black man from the building with the glass door. He would have to work fast and try to finish before the man arrived.

At the first thud of the machete, the birds screamed as though the heavy blade had been aimed at them. He ignored their shrill squawks as he slashed the vine free and chopped it into three-foot lengths.

He was working on the last one when he sensed the approach of the guard. Then he heard him. The man was running heavily along the path toward him.

Moving quickly but without haste, the Jivaro gathered the lengths of vine he had cut and stepped into the shadows. The guard ran past him toward the piercing cries of the birds and the Jivaro stepped back onto the path where he could move fast toward his machine.

Suddenly a huge peacock flapped down from a tree, screaming defiantly, and thudded to the ground directly in his path. He moved to go around the bird and two more dropped to the ground, their topnotches raised in an angry ruff, their beaks open as they vented their fury at the intruder.

The Jivaro backed away and was circling to get away from the birds when a voice shouted, "Hold it right there."

Damn. It was the guard coming toward him with a gun in his hand. The Jivaro was angry at himself for allowing the birds to override his instincts. He did not want to kill this man. He was not an enemy. He would wait until the man was close enough then take the gun from him. Without the gun the man could not harm him.

Then the man saw the machete and his eyes widened. He lifted the barrel of the gun and fired, but the Jivaro had seen the guard's eyes and was already on the ground and rolling. It was too late to escape. If he ran he would never make it to the concealment of the trees. The guard fired twice more before the Jivaro surged to his feet, swinging the machete in a deadly arc that sliced the blade into the back of the man's neck and through his spine. The man made a harsh sound and slumped to the ground, his arms and legs writhing, until the body gave one arching, twisting heave and collapsed.

The Jivaro looked at him in sorrow. He had not wanted to kill. But it was done and now he must take the man's head and perform the *hanlsamata* or the *muisak* would come back to do him harm.

With two blows of the machete he severed the guard's head and threw the machete away. Cradling the pieces of Chando vine with one hand and carrying the head in the other he pushed past the squawking peacocks and ran toward his machine. At the fence he dropped the head and threw the pieces of vine to the other side. He climbed the fence and put the vines on the floor of the machine.

He returned to the fence and stared at the head. For some reason the sight of it repulsed him. Why was that? He was a Jivaro warrior, and yet he dreaded touching this man's head. It was as though some instinct was trying to push through his throbbing pain. Maybe this was a shaman and it was shooting evil darts at him.

He backed away from the fence. He would think about this later. Now he must go before more men came with guns. He got in the machine and drove away. It took all his concentration to find his way back to the house that was his home in this strange city.

Inside the part of the house called a 'kitchen' he stripped the leaves and bark from the Chando vine. He cut the vines into pieces and boiled them in a small amount of water. He sat in a chair staring at nothing, ignoring the pain in his head, until their juices made a brown paste that he mixed with the venom of the black mamba. He smeared the concoction on the steel shafts of the blowgun darts.

Then he went to the bed and lay down. The work had made him more tired than he had ever been. He had to sleep, to prepare for his enemy. But the throbbing would not let him sleep. He wondered if any shaman could make it stop, even though a shaman could often work miracles with potent drugs. The vague memories faded into horrible dreams in which his own shrunken head was worn on a string around the neck of an Acuna warrior, a warrior who looked like the man called Gordo Sanchez.

CHAPTER 9

The L.A. Police Department was so huge and departmentalized that one detective might not know what another was investigating. Even with linked databases it was possible that related cases, unless patiently obvious, might not be correlated until months after they happened—if ever.

Henry Warner was at his desk staring at his notes, but his mind wasn't burdened by the dark shadows of Trejo's death; it was dancing in the warm sunlight of delightful memory. After dinner with Irene his life would never be the same. How could he concentrate on such mundane matters as murder when the memory would be an exquisite joy that drove away all thoughts of mysterious death? Even the strident voices of Detectives Clancy Morgan and Jigger Mulvaney talking about a grisly murder at Descanso Gardens failed to distract him.

Morgan was sitting on the edge of Mulvaney's desk trying to get him to knock off writing the report until after lunch, but Mulvaney continued to scribble. Their words flitted like flies around the honey of Henry's daydream. He was more interested in recapturing the pleasant sensation he experienced when Irene Perez was close to him. There seemed to be an electrical charge that pulled him toward her. At the same time her objectivity told him to keep his distance. She was here for the purpose of assisting him in the case. She had no other interest. So he must not allow the invisible aura to whirl him into a vortex from which he might not escape. But the attraction force, although unseen, had the power of an industrial magnet. He wondered if Irene Perez felt it, too. More likely she felt nothing and he was living in a fantasy of his own making. Then Mulvaney's question penetrated his golden haze.

"How far away from the body was the head?"

Morgan looked over Mulvaney's beefy shoulder. "What the hell are you writing, a book? The head was over by the fence. Just put down its location, not how far the freak carried it."

Henry put down the Trejo file, and walked over to get a look at the report Mulvaney was completing. "What's this about a head?"

"Damn bloody mess, is what," Morgan said. He had recently been transferred from Bunko to Homicide and was not used to the violence yet. With a wave of his hand, he said, "How the hell are we supposed to find a psycho like that?"

"Maybe I can take it off your hands."

"Yeah? Well, last night some nut broke into Descanso Gardens— you know, the botanical gardens. The nut was chopping up a tree when the guard spots him. He kills the guard with a machete. We found it near the body. Then he cuts off the guy's head. He carries it all the goddamned way to the fence."

"He didn't take the head with him?"

"Only as far as the fence for some damn reason. He had a car on the other side."

"Can you imagine a nut like that with a driver's license?" Mulvaney muttered.

"Took some of the wood though," Morgan snorted. "Hell of a damn price to pay for fire wood."

"Maybe he wanted to start his own tree," Mulvaney suggested. "You know. Graft it like they do fruit trees."

"Fruit shit. With him it'd have to be a nut tree."

Mulvaney sniggered. "Hey. You don't suppose it was the same nut who chopped the head off that snake, do you?"

"What snake?" Henry asked. This business of cutting off heads was turning into an epidemic.

Mulvaney said, "Saw it in the paper. Some screwball went in the reptile house at the zoo. Broke one of the cages and killed a snake. Cut off its head."

"Just one snake?"

"Yup. Just one."

"Did they find the head?"

"Nope. They think he took it with him."

"What the shit would anybody want with a snake's head?" Morgan asked.

For some reason, the thought of the decapitated snake made Henry uneasy. "You remember what kind of a snake it was?"

Mulvaney searched his memory. "It was black something. Something like mama."

"From Africa?"

"Yeah. Maybe that's why it was black."

"Black mamba?"

"That's it."

"You know who's got the case?" Henry asked.

"B an' E, I guess," Morgan answered. "As far as I know, killing a snake isn't homicide yet."

"The damn snake deserved it less than a lot of the jerks we see," Mulvaney added.

"You can say that again," Morgan chuckled. "I'm surprised they didn't give the case to us."

"Yeah," Morgan growled. "We get all the nuts."

Henry put aside his interest in the zoo incident. The MO of the killing at the arboretum was too close to that of Trejo to ignore. There might be no connection. On the other hand, suppose it was the beginning of a series? He turned to Morgan. "Where's the body from the arboretum?"

"In the morgue. Woods'll have a lot of fun tryin' to put the pieces together." Henry reached for his jacket, as Morgan added, "Hey. You got something on this?

"I don't know yet. I'll let you know."

Looking at the body on the autopsy table Henry had a feeling of *deja vu.* The man was younger and huskier than Trejo, but the head was missing. Gene Woods had begun his exploratory to determine whether the victim was alive or dead when the head was removed and to pin down the cause of death. As with Trejo, Henry could not see that it mattered much. However, defense attorneys and juries sometimes had peculiar ideas about what constituted the various degrees of murder, so the autopsy had to be thorough, even though it might merely confirm the obvious.

Woods put down the scalpel. "I figured I'd see you sooner or later on this one."

Henry appreciated that Woods had stopped work for him. He had never accustomed his stomach to the sights and smells of an autopsy, and

Gene Woods was perceptive enough to move away from his work when they had to talk, unless it was vital that Henry watch, which thank God, wasn't often. As a senior detective he was able to exercise some control over that. He also knew that if he had been a rookie, especially a female rookie, Woods would have delighted in opening up cavities that required no examination. Henry remembered the time Woods had incapacitated an entire class from the police academy by disemboweling a wino with one flick of his scalpel.

"Where's the head?" he asked.

"Cold storage. You want it?"

"Christ no. I just wanted to make sure you had it."

"You're getting paranoid about heads."

"That might be," Henry admitted. "So why didn't you call me?"

Woods sighed and lit a cigar. "Oh. You interested?"

He puffed on his cigar, making Henry wait. Woods loved this game: make you admit that he was in charge by forcing you to break the silence. When Henry could not hold back any longer he spread his hands in defeat.

"So, do you think there's a connection between this and the Trejo murder?"

Woods thought a moment. "No. This guy was killed with a machete. The killer wasn't after him the way he was Trejo. Or that's what it looks like. I think the head was an afterthought."

"What the hell was he doing out there?"

Woods stared at him woodenly. "He was a guard. Didn't they tell you?"

Henry sighed. "Okay, Doc. What was the *killer* doing out there?"

Woods smiled and waved his cigar. This is what he had been leading up to the entire time. "What am I, a magician? Even a ventriloquist couldn't make this guy talk."

"Jesus, Doc. Whoever heard of a comedian pathologist? You guys are supposed to be all cotton swabs and rubber gloves."

Woods shrugged. "Ask a stupid question..."

Henry enjoyed sparring with Woods, but right now he was short of time. There might even be some connection between this murder and the killing of the snake at the zoo. An idea shot through his mind with the joyous impact of spring sunshine. Maybe Irene Perez would have some ideas about this.

The thought of seeing Irene even sooner than he had planned increased his desire to come directly to the point: "No clues on the body that would tie the two together?"

"None I could see."

"Okay, Doc. Have fun."

He was turning away when Woods said, "Damn job's killing my feet. I think I'll go into private practice."

At the door, Henry looked back. "Who needs a private pathologist?"

"You've got a point." Woods picked up a scalpel and turned back to the body of the guard. "Okay. Come on, fella. Talk to me."

Henry called Irene Perez and asked if she would like to accompany him to the site of the botanical gardens murder. When she hesitated, he explained that it might have some connection with the Trejo case and she agreed to go with him.

An hour later he was impatiently waiting for her in the atrium-like hotel lobby. When she stepped out of the elevator he was again warmed by her elegant beauty. In preparation for the gardens she was wearing a white knit sweater decorated with colorful broad bands, long, white pants and low-heeled, white shoes that had a delicate pink stripe running from the toe to the heel. Her hair was caught up in a long pony-tail and topped with a soft newsboy's cap. A white bag hung from her shoulder on a long golden chain. She smiled and said his name, making it sound as though she was delighted to be meeting the most important person in the world, and he knew that every man in the place was watching him with envy. As they walked toward the door she clung to his arm with both hands and Henry resisted an urge to look back over his shoulder with a smug smile. He could easily become addicted to the feeling. Threading his car through the early afternoon traffic north on Hill Street toward the Pasadena Freeway Henry told Irene everything he knew about the murder at the arboretum. "There may be no connection with Trejo, but there are enough similarities I thought we should check it out."

Irene sat forward in the seat. "The body. Is it still there?"

"Oh, no. That was removed this morning."

She relaxed with a look of embarrassment. "I'm sorry. I've never become used to death."

"I wish I wasn't. But I'm afraid it has become very impersonal. I'm not sure I like the feeling."

"You think you are becoming, hmm, insensitive?"

"Something like that."

"Perhaps it is best that you are."

"I don't think it's a matter of best. It's nature helping the psyche adapt. Protecting it, I guess. Like people who work in a strong odor environment get to the point where they don't even smell it. Or prostitutes get to the point where they're indifferent to what they do."

"But learning to adapt in one area doesn't make you insensitive in others."

"I hope not." He grinned at her, wanting to break the heavy mood. "I still like flowers and ice cream."

She returned the smile, studying his profile as he concentrated on his driving. "And puppies and kittens, too, I'll bet." She caught her lower lips in her teeth. "And children?"

He lifted his hand from the wheel. "All except the brats. Them I can do without."

"Brats? What are 'brats'?"

"'Spoiled brats' is the proper expression."

"Oh. I think I understand. No one enjoys spoiled brats."

"When I have kids," Henry said, "I'll love them, but I wouldn't like them to be spoiled rotten."

"Would you beat them?" Irene asked with a chiding smile.

"I don't think you have to beat kids if you gain their respect early. If you wait too long, it could be too late."

"Respect? What about love?"

"You can't have love without respect."

Irene raised and eyebrow. "I suppose it's a question of which comes first."

"They're linked together like, uh…"

"Love and marriage?"

He wished he knew whether there was anything implied in her answer. "Yeah. Like love and marriage."

She leaned back in the seat, curling her legs under her. For the first time in years, Henry found himself caring about making the right impression.

That he was having such thoughts should have amused him, but it was hard to find humor in something that might influence the remainder of his life.

At the arboretum they were given directions at the information center, and as they walked toward the murder site, Henry was sorry they had to be among the sun-speckled trees and the dappled pathway on such an unpleasant mission. He would like to be walking with this lady on a Sunday afternoon carrying a picnic basket and not worrying about a thing except whether or not there were going to be ants. He was debating about whether to make a try at holding her hand when he was saved from making a fool of himself by the sight of a uniformed policeman seated in a garden chair. He stood up when he saw them approaching.

"Sorry, folks," he said. "You'll have to take another path."

Henry showed him his badge. "I'm Lieutenant Warner. Okay if we look around?"

The patrolmen knew that Henry did not have to ask his permission and he smiled, appreciating the courtesy. "Yes, sir. Go right ahead." He pointed to an area that had been outlined by chalk-dust. In the center was a large, ugly stain. "That's where they found the body. Not much to see."

Henry tried to visualize what might have happened. Irene moved to look at the remains of the vine that the killer had destroyed.

"That vine the only thing he touched?" Henry asked.

"Yes, sir. He got the machete out of the tool shed. Tore the lock right off."

Henry stared at the trees. The path did not seem to be as well used as some of the others and was located in a relatively remote part of the arboretum. He turned to Irene. "This place is kind of out of the way. He must have been looking for that particular vine."

"It would seem so."

He noticed a small plaque at the base of the vine. He took out his pad and pencil and bent down to copy the name. *Chandorendron tomentosum; Brazil.*

"And Ecuador. It's a reasonably common vine in the Montaña region."

Henry's interest centered on what she was saying. "The Montaña? The upper Amazon basin."

"That's right. In Ecuador."

"Why would he want this particular vine? What good is it?"

"It would make an interesting conversation piece in somebody's garden."

"Oh?" Henry studied her face, trying to phantom what was going on behind those lovely dark eyes. "Why is that?"

"It's one of the vines the natives use to make curare poison for their blowgun darts. The Jivaros call it ampi."

Henry felt his face stiffen. "You mean headhunters?"

Her expression was blank. "Well, yes."

Henry felt a tingle of excitement. "Could a native have done this?"

She looked at the dark stain on the ground. "What you're suggesting...it isn't possible."

"Would it be possible for somebody to make curare out of the stolen parts of the vine?"

"If the person knew how."

"Would the poison be strong enough to kill a man?"

Irene stared at the mutilated remains of the vine. "No. Curare is a powerful muscle relaxant. On a blowgun dart it can immobilize an animal as large as a tapir. But it wouldn't kill it. The hunter would finish it off with a machete." As if drawn by a magnet her eyes again turned toward the stain on the ground.

A thought that had been in the back of Henry's mind came into focus with mild shock. "If the curare was mixed with snake venom," he said softly, "would it be strong enough then?"

Irene looked at him, her dark eyebrows drawn into a frown. "What kind of snake?"

"A black mamba."

Her puzzled look froze as though she were holding her breath. "Curare and mamba venom. I'm no herpetologist, of course, but my guess is that such a mixture could easily kill a human—and quickly."

Henry felt a little sick. He was already thinking that their killer was a psycho. Now it looked as though the psycho had armed himself with a deadly weapon. And for what purpose? What reason could there be except to kill people? But there was always the hope that there was no connection between the cases, and the killer had wanted the vine for some other purpose. The guard had simply been unlucky; he had confronted a thief who had panicked, and it had cost him his life. But why had the killer cut off the head? And carried it away? It didn't make sense.

"Could you tell us," he asked the patrolman, "where they found the guard's head?"

"Yes, sir." The patrolman pointed. "Straight down that path to the fence. You'll see it. It's cordoned off." Henry thanked him and turned to leave with Irene. "Oh, Lieutenant. Do I…uh…have to stay here all night?"

Henry looked around at the strange vine-tangled bushes and trees and the shifting shadows. He wouldn't be overjoyed at spending the night here, guarding a bloodstain made by a maniac. But he didn't want to make the officer feel that he questioned his courage.

"I'll send somebody to keep you company. Too hard to stay awake here alone."

"Yes, sir. I'd probably nod off," he grinned, "in about a week."

Henry and Irene skirted the bloodstain as they moved down the path. Henry glanced once more at the mangled ruins of the vine. If the killer had planned to make curare from the vine, and if it was the same person who had killed the snake, his next victim would not be an accidental killing or one performed in a fit of rage; it would be premeditated murder.

Walking beside him, Irene made a fluttering motion with her hands. "I just cannot believe it was an Indio."

"All the evidence points that way."

"He could not be here. It would be like being killed in the jungle by an Eskimo."

"Or," Henry said dryly, "the Titanic being sunk by an iceberg."

They walked to the place where the killer had climbed the fence. The base of the fence was cordoned off with police banners although there was no patrolman on guard. The lab men had already done their work. Plaster casts had been made of the footprints where the man had jumped down from the fence and an attempt had been made to lift prints from the wire. Henry doubted that they would get enough off the thin strands to be of any use. There were enough bloodstained blades of grass near the fence to indicate where the guard's head had been left. Irene voiced the thought that was going through Henry's mind.

"He went to all the trouble to carry the head this far. I wonder why he didn't take it away with him?"

"The man who killed Trejo did the same thing: took it as far as the gate, then left it."

"It's as if he changed his mind."

"Yes. What would make him do that?"

"Maybe someone saw him. He had to run."

"That might have been true at Trejo's, but not here."

"You mean because of the chando vine. If he had time to take it with him he must have had time to take the head."

Henry couldn't hold back a smile; she was so quick at deductive reasoning. He couldn't count the number of supposedly intelligent people who couldn't work out the most obvious syllogism. He wondered what other surprises might be behind those lovely eyes.

"How would you like to make a trip to the zoo?"

He knew that she would know the reason for the trip, so he wasn't surprised when she nodded. "I was going to suggest it." As they walked back to the car, she asked, "How did you make a connection between what happened here and the zoo?"

How could he explain the tedious process of putting bits and pieces together, then coming up with an answer, which might very well be wrong. So he shrugged modestly. "A hunch. I'm not sure there is a connection."

"Do you have these 'hunches' often?"

"Hardly ever. I prefer to deal with facts."

"The way a detective should."

"The way he should if he wants his evidence to hold up in court."

She looked at him, and he thought he saw a dancing in her eyes that meant she had found out something about him. He wondered what it was. He'd have to be more careful. If he wanted to impress her as an intellectual, but one with panache, he'd better watch his syntax. No point in giving away his true boring personality before she'd hardly learned his name. She'd find out soon enough.

The route back toward L.A. took them past the turnoff on Zoo Drive at the Ventura/Golden State Freeway interchange and he parked near the administration building. The assistant manager of the zoo showed them where the glass cage for the snake had been shattered. He was a slender, balding man with the fine blonde hair of many Scandinavians. He took off wire-rimmed glasses and scrubbed them with a snowy white handkerchief.

"It's so ludicrous. We've had break-ins before and animals have been killed or brutalized, but never the reptiles. People are afraid of them; at least, the miscreant personalities who are so mentally unstable that they would mutilate an animal. Frankly, I wouldn't weep if the culprit had been bitten."

Henry studied the broken glass and the name on the front of the case. "*Black Mamba; Africa.* I understand it's extremely dangerous."

The assistant manager sniffed. "That's putting it mildly."

The snake lay on the floor of the cage. Flies attracted by the odor, crusted the dried blood. Henry turned away. "I never saw a snake that long except a boa or an anaconda."

Irene Perez avoided the grisly scene, as she peered at the snakes in the other cages. Now she looked up. "Mambas can grow to a length of more than four meters. Their bite is almost one-hundred percent fatal."

"Fourteen feet?" Henry whistled. "It took guts to break that cage."

"Not if you're insane," the assistant manager said. "The culprit might not have known it was venomous."

"I seriously doubt that," Irene said.

The assistant manager asked, "What makes you think so?"

She nodded toward the other cages. "He passed these in favor of that one. If he wanted a trophy he could have taken any of them. Most are much more colorful, exotic." She looked at Henry. "I think you were right. He was after the venom."

"I shudder to think what he might do with it," the assistant manager said.

Henry asked, "Is there a market for that sort of thing?"

"For mamba antivenin? I doubt it."

"The mamba is a member of the cobra family, genus Dendroaspis," Irene said. "And cobra venom is used for the manufacture of antivenin. But there is enough available. I doubt that there would be a market for it even if the thief knew where to go."

"So," Henry said, "he either took the head and didn't know or care about the venom. Or he was after the venom."

"I think it was a cult," the assistant manager said. "They're all insane. They might need the head for one of their satanic rituals."

"And your guards didn't see any one?"

"No. Some of the animals were extremely nervous. They sensed the intruders. The guards were investigating the disturbance when they heard the glass break. By the time they got here, the intruders were gone."

"You think it was more than one person?"

"Cults usually are."

"I believe it was one person," Irene said.

Henry sighed with deep satisfaction. "Why do you say that?"

"If it was a cult they would have taken the entire snake, most likely, alive. And even if they'd killed it, they would have taken the body."

In her intensity her eyes glowed and her hands moved like graceful birds. Henry could have watched her all day.

"We'll probably never know for sure," he said. "unless we find the head on somebody's mantel."

As he led the way outside the assistant manager sniffed. "When can we clean up here? We are running a zoo for the people, you know."

Henry thought about the workload at headquarters. B and E were probably similarly loaded. They had already completed their examination of the site. He could imagine how much additional effort they would put into trying to find out who killed a snake. "Any time," he said. "I believe the other detectives have enough to go on."

Leaving the zoo grounds Henry had no eyes for the animals they passed. His entire thought process was focused on constructing a solid relationship between the stolen curare vines and the snake. Could they have been done by the same person? His instinct told him they were.

"Please, Mr. Warner. Not so fast."

He became aware that Irene was struggling to keep up with him. "I'm sorry. I guess I got carried away."

"You were charging like a wolf after a sheep," she exclaimed. "Do you always do that when you're thinking?"

"I don't know," Henry admitted with a smile. "I never had anyone with me before."

"No wonder. They probably couldn't keep up."

"Sorry. I'll try not to think with such intensity."

"Did you arrive at any conclusion?"

"Only that the killer is leading up to something. And I can't think of a single thing we can do that will head him off."

"Perhaps it is finished. Perhaps these things were only the work of vandals and we will never know who did such monstrous things."

For once, Henry thought she was wrong. The chances of the killer not striking again were about as thin as the razor sharp blade of the mad man's knife.

CHAPTER 10

The shaman was angry. He glared at the Jivaro warrior and shook his finger. The warrior was deathly afraid that the shaman would hurl darts at him from his open mouth, and they would go straight into his heart and the shaman would then pull his soul from his head and send it into the night to wander endlessly. And all because he had almost made a mistake in making the ampi poison.

When the shaman allowed him to continue he worked with more caution, carefully mixing the ampi with the snake venom, then smearing the thick paste on the blowgun darts. Only when the shaman grunted his satisfaction had the exhausted warrior been allowed to go to bed where he sank into a sleep that was shot through with the faces of his enemies, especially the one he knew he had to kill very soon.

For the first time in his life Steve Kelly was too sick to go to work. He had awakened late wondering why he had not heard the alarm. He started to get up and stifled a groan. The headache pain was coursing down his spine, radiating through his body. He felt totally drained; the simple act of swinging his legs off the bed was an effort.

The doctor at Quito had told him he would have periods of fatigue and pain, but he hadn't been told that they would become worse. Maybe that's why he had been given the name of the doctor in L.A. Where had he put the card? He should go see the guy. Maybe he could give him a pill or a shot that would kill the pain. He rummaged through the drawers of his dresser where he threw old papers and letters he wanted to save, and he felt a brief satisfaction when he found the card. The name on it was Dr. Hector Gutierrez. The address was on Alverado.

Steve held the card, considering what to do. He was feeling better since he got up. Maybe all he needed was a couple of aspirin. If this Gutierrez was a cutter he might want to operate or something. He sure as hell didn't want some quack cutting into his brain. Then he was shaken by a new thought: suppose the guy was a psychiatrist. Maybe they thought he was going crazy. That would explain the crazy dreams. And the dart and the blowgun. If he was losing his mind this Dr. Gutierrez might have him locked up. He couldn't stand that.

A couple of aspirin would fix him up. If he had to he'd take the whole damned bottle.

Moving painfully, he made his way into the kitchen. First he needed a strong cup of coffee. He was reaching for the jar of instant when his body went rigid with shock. What the shit? The kitchen was a mess. Bits of wood and shredded leaves littered the sink and floor. In a saucepan the remains of a dark substance was hardening. An empty, filthy butter container was lying on the floor, oozing some milky white substance.

His eyes focused on a row of steel darts that were arranged on the drain board, their tips smeared with more of the dark substance. He touched his finger to the substance and sniffed it. The odor was faintly familiar. He touched it to the tip of his tongue. Ampi. And something else. Snake venom. You needed the combination to kill an enemy like Gordo Sanchez.

Damn that Sanchez anyway. The pain had started with him. Maybe there was a purpose for the blowgun and the darts. Maybe he had been sent to this country to find his enemy and kill him. Now that he had the poisoned darts it would be done. He was putting them in the leather pouch when he became aware of a ringing sound. It was coming from the instrument he knew was a telephone. He was supposed to pick it up. He did so.

"Steve?"

Steve? That's right. He was Steve Kelly. He rubbed his hand across his face. "Helen? Yeah, it's me."

"You sound so strange."

"I guess I'm picking up a cold." How could he explain that he couldn't remember what he as doing before the phone rang?

There was a brief pause. "Are you sure that's all it is?"

Anger pierced the throbbing in his temples. "What's that supposed to mean?"

"Well, your headaches. I was afraid—"

"I'm okay," he interrupted. "I'm okay."

Again there was a pause. "I was worried. You didn't come to work. Not even a call."

Steve hated to lie, especially to Helen. But he couldn't tell her the truth. Not about the dreams and not about finding the blowgun and the ampi-coated darts. Ampi? Why had he thought of that strange word?

"Steve?" Helen pleaded.

"I'm sorry, honey. I just thought of something and I had to, uh, write it down."

Real concern was in her voice. "I was thinking about last night and, don't get mad, but I do wish you'd see a doctor, even if it is only a bad cold."

"Yeah. Okay." He glanced at the card on his dresser. "I've got the name of one right here. Doctor Gutierrez."

"Are you going today?"

He looked at his watch and it was already four o'clock. "It's kind of late now. Look. If I'm not feeling better in the morning, I'll go see him before I come to work. I promise."

"You really promise?"

"Yeah. Cross my heart." He was acutely conscious of the pounding in his head that went on and on.

"I think I should come over and fix you some dinner. Have you eaten anything?"

"No." He would never be able to get rid of the mess in the kitchen before she got here. "I mean, don't come over. I don't want to give you this cold. I can fix something. I've got plenty of stuff here."

"All right. But you call me in the morning if you go to work or not. Okay?"

"Okay. And, Helen, I'll be okay."

"You'd better be." Her voice softened. "The next time we get together I want you healthy."

"Right. That's another promise." Steve chuckled, loving her more than ever. "Okay, honey. I'll call you in the morning."

He hung up the phone and stared at it. Should he tell her about the nightmares? No. She would never understand. Shit. He didn't understand them himself. She might not even believe they were nightmares. But what the hell else could they be? Even though there was that blood he'd found on his pants. And the blowgun and darts. If she knew about them, what would she think? Worse, what would she do? Probably call a psychiatrist— or the cops. She was right about one thing. If he didn't feel better in the morning he was going to see that doctor. He couldn't take much more. It wasn't just the stabbing pain, it was the awful dreams. They worried him more than the possible reason for the pain, which—he was afraid to think— might be cancer. God, if that were true it would have to be cancer of his brain.

He dismissed the thought. He was too young, too tough to let some bug kill him. He would rustle up an early dinner and hit the sack. A good nights sleep would fix him up. To make sure he would sleep he walked two blocks to a liquor store and bought another bottle of aspirin and a fifth of Jack Daniels. Liquor always made him sleep; old Jack wouldn't let him down.

But the aspirin and liquor only dulled the throbbing that started in his head and pulsed through his body. When he managed to drift into a drugged sleep his dreams were filled with images of thick jungles and blowgun hunts with painted warriors and silent journeys to long houses to kill an enemy and take his head. That was what the shaman told him he must do. He would never be free of pain until his enemy was dead and the *hanlsamata* had been performed.

He felt stiff and numb when the warrior rose from the strange bed and pulled on the familiar pants and shoes. However bad he felt he had to find his enemy. He picked up his blowgun, and grunted when he observed the ampi on the darts. He had done a good job. The shaman would be pleased. He fixed the packet of darts to his belt. Before he went out into the night, he took a sharp knife from a drawer in the cooking room and thrust it under his belt. He wished he had a machete. It would be a better weapon if he was unable to kill his enemy with the blowgun.

Outside, the moon was a huge smog-reddened disc low on the horizon. The night simmered in the heat that the Santa Ana wind had swept in from the Mojave Desert during the day. He got into the machine and made the journey to the house of his enemy. He knew where it was. At one time in the dim past he had taken one of the men from a construction project to the house of the man called Sanchez. It was near a park called 'Elysian'. That was good. There would be trees and other forms of cover in the park.

When he located the house he drove past, studying the surroundings. It was a small frame bungalow set back from the street. Two old machines without wheels were rusting in the weed-choked front yard. The yard behind the house bordered on the park where there were many trees. An attempt had been made to grow a lawn, but it was now matted into clumps of weedy patches in dirt and dust. Sanchez's truck was parked in the rear yard next to a shiny 1967 Chevrolet Monte Carlo.

He stopped his machine at a cross street that dead-ended in the trees. He turned off the engine and sat for a moment in the deep quietness. Except for the muted undertone of the city the night was sleeping. Taking the blowgun, he moved into the shadows beneath the trees where he circled up behind the house of his enemy. As silent as the lingering heat he moved through the trees. Every house he passed had one or more dogs tied in the back yard, and he drifted farther back into the shadows. Sanchez would probably also have a dog, and maybe that was good. He was trying to think of a way to get his enemy out of his house and the dog could help. Only the most foolish warrior would go into an enemy's house to kill him.

No. The enemy should be lured into the open. The best way was to make his dog bark. But if the victim was smart he wouldn't come out until he was sure it was not a trap. And he would also bring other warriors with him so that he would be safe from attack by any but a large group. Still Sanchez was not wise to the ways of the jungle, and perhaps he could be brought out by the dog. Then he would have to be killed quickly or other people might come out of the house. And he wanted Sanchez alone. This place was filled with strange people, unknown spirits, hidden dangers. If he could not kill his enemy without being seen it might be better to wait for another time.

He studied the yard of Sanchez from the cover of the trees. After a moment he saw the dog. It was a Doberman tied to the front bumper of a truck. The dog's head was lifted, its pointed ears slanted forward, searching for the sensory intrusion that had brought it awake. It got up in one fluid motion and stood stiff-legged, his teeth bared, growling deep in its throat, staring toward the trees.

The warrior picked up a twig and snapped it. The Doberman went wild, lunging at the end of his rope and voicing a series of penetrating barks as chilling as the sight of his bared fangs. Other dogs recognized the certainty in the warning, and the neighborhood erupted in a frenzy of violent barking. The warrior waited, patient as dust. He hoped that his enemy would come out quickly before others located the source of the disturbance and converge. If that happened he would have to leave, and he wanted this ended now so that the pain in his head would go away

A light came on in the house of his enemy and the warrior tensed. He raised his blowgun to silence the dog, then hesitated. The dog was not his enemy. There was no reason to kill him as long as the rope securing him was strong and did not break.

Sanchez came out on the porch at the rear of the house and stopped. His only clothing was a pair of baggy shorts and his hairy belly slopped over them like an obscene balloon. But his bare arms and huge chest indicated his strength. He carried a shotgun in his two hands, the muzzle raised. He stood on the porch behind one of the wooden posts and stared across the yard, his small eyes probing for the reason his dog was barking.

The warrior swung the blowgun for his shot. At the instant he fired Sanchez moved toward the steps. The dart went past his head with a whisper and thudded into the door jamb where it vibrated like the tongue of a deadly snake. Sanchez jerked his head around, unable to see the dart clearly in the darkness.

"What the shit?" He raised his voice at the dog, "Chocho! *Que pasa? Que pasa?*" When the dog continued its frenzied barking, Sanchez crouched in the darkness and yelled, "Chocho! *Callete!*"

The warrior raised the blowgun for another shot. But Sanchez was now partially concealed by the porch railing. It was a bad shot and Sanchez was a dangerous man. It was best to kill him quickly. One did not kill an enemy for the satisfaction of watching him die. An enemy was killed because he was trying to kill you. And a quick death meant less danger to you. He had to draw Sanchez out into the open where he could get a clean shot.

The warrior stepped into the yard. The dog exploded in a frenzy of snarling and barking, snapping at the rope that was preventing him from destroying the intruder. Sanchez took a step off the porch to see the reason. He looked at the dog. Then his eyes swung, and he saw the Jivaro warrior. He was lifting the shotgun when the warrior fired his dart. It streaked across the yard, and with a faint thud, buried itself between Sanchez's eyes.

¶ For an instant Sanchez stood frozen, his eyes wide. Then he released the shotgun and his fingers clawed at the plug protruding from his forehead, frantically attempting to pull the six inches of poisoned steel from his brain. He succeeded in yanking the plug free, but the steel spike was held by the bone in a vice-like grip and in seconds his fingers, nerveless from the fast working ampi, trembled while his arms beat the air as he tried to raise them. His mouth dropped open, emitting groans of frustrated rage. He staggered, performing a dance of death before he fell to one knee then toppled like a butchered steer. He struggled to rise, gasping for breath as the curare and poison worked on the nerve-centers of his brain. But even his powerful arms could not push him up, his legs twitching in an insane compulsion to resist the approach of death.

Then the strength went out of him and he lay trembling on the earth. His legs gave a last convulsive kick and his breath escaped in an explosive grunt that lifted a faint puff of dust. Only his hands moved, his fingers fluttering against the ground with a dying caress. Then he was still, his open eyes staring through a film.

The warrior took the knife from his belt and went to Sanchez. Ignoring the frantic dog he cut off the head of his enemy. He had just finished when the door of the house opened and he heard a woman's voice: "Carlos?"

She saw the Jivaro standing in the moonlight with the bloody knife in one hand and the head of his enemy in the other and her scream was a thin moaning cry torn from her throat. He could have killed her, but she was not his enemy. Instead, he thrust the knife back under his belt, scooped up his blowgun, and ran into the darkness. Moving fast he circled through the trees to the machine, followed by a new tone in the screams of the woman as she focused on the body of her man.

He stopped in the moonlight at the edge of the trees and used the knife to make a slit down the back of the head. The lights in other houses were beginning to come on as he peeled the skin away from the bone. When the entire skull had been freed he tossed it aside. Carefully he pulled the skin together, forming it into a small package so that the *muisak* soul would not escape. He would like to build a fire and do the preparation of the *tsantsa*, but soon there would be many friends of his enemy here. So he put the head and his blowgun in the machine and drove away. He was very careful driving back to his house so that the men whose duty it was to enforce the laws of the white men would not stop him.

In the cooking area of the house there was a machine to make fire. There was plenty of hot water from the pipe with the handle on top, and after he'd scraped away the excess flesh from inside the skin, he used the hot water to wash the skin thoroughly. In another part of the house he found good needles and strong thread which he used to sew up the slit in the back and to sew together the eyes and the mouth, making a pouch of the skin.

Now he needed something to make the skin shrink. He did not have rocks and pebbles that should be heated and placed inside the pouch. Nor did he have sand to heat and place inside for the final curing. He would have to find a substitute. He went to the place where the tools were kept and found a number of small, round steel balls. Inside he heated them in an iron skillet and began the long process of placing the hot steel balls inside the bag of skin while he worked the flesh with his hands to help it retain its shape as the heat drove out the moisture. And as the skin dried it shrank.

For the final heating and shaping he mixed salt and rice together and heated the mixture in a skillet until it was burning hot. He poured the mixture into the pouch of skin, which had shrunken to the size of a grapefruit. He tied the neck shut.

Using a strong piece of string he then tied it to the hair and suspended the *tsantsa* above a low gas flame of the cooking machine for the final drying. He wished he had charcoal to rub on the skin so that the *muisak* soul inside could not see him. Even so, this *tsantsa* would do very well for the *hanlsamata* that he would perform when the time was right. Then his enemy would no longer fling evil darts into him and the pain in his head and body would go away.

The pain was still with him when he went into the room with the bed, but it did not seem as bad and he was able to go to sleep thinking that the pain would soon be gone. And in his dreams he saw the head of his enemy stuck on a pole in a jungle clearing, outlined by the flickering light of a fire. Around the pole he and other Jivaro warriors danced the *hanlsamata*, killing the soul of his enemy forever.

CHAPTER II

When the call came at 4:00 AM it jolted Henry Warner out of a deep sleep. There had been another killing in which the victim's head was severed. Henry rolled out of bed with a groan. He had never been able to get out of bed feeling bright and peppy. Well, there had been that a period from the age of five to eight when he vaguely remembered flinging himself into the day with total abandonment based upon complete ignorance of the day's ability to deal misfortune. The wisdom that bad luck was always waiting in ambush had been slow in coming. But its slowness had ingrained the lesson well: get up slow and be prepared for the worst. Thank heavens he'd put that brief halcyon period behind him.

Of course, if he ever got more than four or five hours of sleep it might help him face the day with something akin to enthusiasm. As it was his legs had to work hard to shuffle into the bathroom where his eyes, peering at him from the mirror, beseeched him for more time in the closed position. But his mind was wide awake, remembering last night's movie and dinner with Irene Perez.

The movie was forgettable, but he would never be free of the memory of sitting across from her during dinner. Once again he was reminded of the suggestion that the most dangerous element of a relationship was sexual intercourse. Sexual passion might require a certain commitment, but it was shallow. Conversation was infinitely more dangerous. Sex was transitory; conversation had staying power. An hour of sex, however marvelous, was not nearly as hazardous to one's independence as an hour of delightful conversation. You married someone you could talk to.

He stared at the face in the mirror. Marriage. Children. Was he ready for that? Was any man ever ready? The fact that he was even thinking about it was frightening. It might be a good idea if he curtailed his time with her. It was increasingly evident that he was becoming addicted. When it came to this woman, there was nothing to that old saying that 'familiarity breeds contempt.'

But with this new killing, how could he stay away from her? He needed her expertise, which meant he would have to be with her for several more dangerous hours. He could make a preliminary investigation without her. There might be no connection between this case and the others. A person's head could be cut off for any number of reasons. It might be better for both of them if he handled this one alone.

She answered on the tenth ring, sounding sexily sleepy. When he mentioned the latest murder she said that she would be ready when he got there to pick her up.

Despite the early hour she looked rested, moving with the assured grace of a competent woman at peace with her beauty and her intellect. When she saw Henry, she smiled as though she enjoyed seeing him again. He reminded himself not to read any significance into it; she probably greeted every colleague with the same warmth. She had a compassionate nature.

For a moment he allowed himself to enjoy the illusion that he was a little special to her. Then he sighed as reality closed in. He was simply a rusty freighter passing a beautiful yacht and would soon be forgotten in the wake of time.

The sun was edging the horizon, its rays turning the city haze golden brown when Henry and Irene pulled up beside the gaggle of black-and-whites at the western edge of Elysian Park. One of the patrolmen directed them to the rear of a run-down bungalow where they found Gene Woods standing near a plastic body-covering. He was talking to a uniformed captain Henry recognized as Paul Rodriguez of Rampart Division. The coroner's car was pulled up near a beat-up truck, and two men with a gurney were standing beside a coroner's ambulance waiting for Woods to finish his investigation. The bloodstain that had soaked into the dust was the biggest Henry had ever seen. But it went with the odd shape under the plastic cover, which was flat where the head should have been. Most of the uniformed officers were searching around the house and in the trees behind the buildings while every dog in the neighborhood barked incessantly. Near the house a knot of Latinos huddled together, chattering in Spanish.

"Hello, Gene," Henry said. "Hi, Paul. *Que paso?*"

"You mean *pasa*," Captain Rodriguez said, with a shake of his head. He saw Irene Perez and the scowl left his face. Irene had that effect on people.

"Dr. Perez," he said. "This is Captain Rodriguez. I believe you know Gene Woods."

They said hello and Rodriguez took Irene's hand. "Dr. Perez. I've heard of you. You're working with Henry on the Trejo killing."

"I'm trying." Her flashing smile had its usual effect. Even Gene Woods looked pleasant. "But I'm afraid I have not been of much help."

"Yes, she has," Henry corrected. "We're getting some solid leads."

"Well, you should get some good ones here," Gene Woods said laconically.

Captain Rodriguez stifled a yawn. "Why the hell don't people kill each other in the daytime so we can get some sleep?"

Henry had often wondered the same thing. "An interesting point. My theory is that it has something to do with man's fear of the dark."

Gene Woods, as usual, took the opposite view. "So why are most nefarious rites conducted in the dark of the night? The darker the better."

"So why are so many based upon the time of the full moon?" Henry countered.

"Because they have to see, and because even the bad guys are afraid of the dark."

"Jesus." Rodriguez smiled at Irene. "Never ask a rhetorical question around pseudo-intellectuals."

"Maybe they both read the same book."

Gene Woods chuckled. "I did. I've never been able to prove that Henry can read."

"If I couldn't," Henry answered, "I'd have become a medical examiner instead of a first class detective."

Woods snorted and winked at Irene. "First? At the rate you're working, you couldn't come in first in a turtle race."

Henry felt a pang of resentment. He knew that Gene Woods was joking, but like so many jokes it was based on truth. He wasn't working very fast. In fact, he hadn't been getting anywhere with his investigation. He had a familiar sense of being helpless. He was a representative of one of the most powerful law enforcement machines in the world, yet he felt as ineffective as an old mouse in a new maze. It was especially galling because he wanted to impress Irene Perez as a competent, capable detective. Well, maybe this new killing would help him turn a few corners.

A shotgun was lying next to the body and he hooked a finger in its trigger guard and picked it up. He sniffed the barrel. It had not been fired. He replaced it exactly as he'd found it, and turned to Gene Woods. "What killed him?"

"Can't be sure. No conclusive marks on the body. What there is of it." He turned to Captain Rodriguez. "Paul, do you have that blowgun dart we found?"

Henry's pulse leaped. Blowgun? He glanced at Irene and saw that she was as startled he was. He watched in fascination as Rodriguez took a plastic-wrapped object from an envelope. Henry held his breath as he unwrapped it. The object was a six inches long steel dart with a round plug on the back end made of some soft material, possibly cork. The needle-like point and shaft were smeared with a dark, sticky substance that Henry would bet his life was a mixture of curare and snake venom.

"Could something like this have killed him?" he asked Gene Woods.

Woods shrugged, "If it hit him in the right place."

Henry handed the dart to Irene, leaving it in the plastic. "What do you think, Doctor?"

Irene held it at the base of the thin shaft, and sniffed the substance. "I think this is coated with a combination of curare and venom. It would kill no matter where it hit."

"I didn't see any sign of a hit on the body," Woods said.

Henry looked at the body. The plastic covering was flat where the head should have been making it look macabre. "On what you have, you mean?"

"Obviously." There was a touch of annoyance in Woods' voice.

Irene touched between her eyes. "The preferred spot is here." She touched the side of her neck. "Or here. In the vein."

Woods stared at her. "In the vein? That would take a hell of a marksman."

She gave him a tight smile. "Indeed."

Woods looked crestfallen and Henry grinned. Served Woods right.

He needed to be put in his place once in a while.

Irene gestured toward the body. "May I see?"

Woods' eyebrows lifted. Henry could almost read his mind: Woods couldn't believe that a woman so sleekly beautiful would want to look at such a grisly object. He wasn't surprised when Woods grinned. "Go ahead."

She squatted at the edge of the bloodstain and lifted the plastic to look at the severed neck. Her face was impassive as she peered at the raw, ugly flesh. She might have been looking at a dead fish in a market. When she let the plastic drop and straightened the three men waited for her to say something but she was silent, her forehead drawn into a frown of concentration.

Finally, Henry asked, "Well?"

She had worry in her eyes. "It has the typical appearance of the work of a native."

"A head hunter?"

Irene shook her head. "It's not possible. How could he survive here?"

"But it does have the characteristics?" Gene Woods asked.

"Yes. But it could be coincidence. There is not a great difference in the way a native of the Montaña would remove a head and the way it might be done by anyone."

"I suppose not," Woods admitted. "I don't see that many."

Henry turned to Rodriguez. "No witnesses, I suppose."

Rodriguez said, "One. His wife."

That was a break. Maybe he could at last get a description that would mean something. "Where is she?"

Rodriquez motioned toward the people on the back porch of the house. "In the house."

Henry turned to Irene. "I'd better talk to her." He turned toward the house, then stopped. "What was his name?"

"Sanchez. Carlos Sanchez. They called him Gordo."

"She speak English?"

Rodriguez made a small shrug. "Some."

"Would you like me to go with you?" Irene asked.

Henry could have taken Captain Rodriguez, but he liked the idea of having Irene with him. The woman was probably very distraught and might be more inclined to talk to another woman. "If you don't mind. My Spanish is *muy malo.*"

At their approach the group of people on the porch moved aside. They were Latinos dressed as though they had been in a hurry. Henry wondered how many of the children belonged to Sanchez and how they would survive now that their father was dead. Too bad there wasn't some way to make the killer take over the responsibility for a family when he killed the breadwinner. It would make a hell of a deterrent if a killer knew he would have to support about ten kids and a widow for the rest of his life. As it was, the killer might get twenty-five years to life, which meant parole in five or six years, then he could go his merry way while the victim's family suffered for years. But that was the system and there wasn't a hell of a lot he could do about it.

The kitchen was clean to the point of being antiseptic; no sign of roaches or peeling walls. The white paint on the cupboards was chipped and faded, but it had been scoured almost to the bare wood. The tiles on the sink and the linoleum on the floor gleamed in the brilliance of fluorescent lights paneled in the ceiling. There was the faint odor of Pine Sol cleaner. So much for stereotypes.

The sound of sobbing came through a door leading to a hallway. In the hall, there were places on the worn carpet where a valiant attempt had been made to scrub out spots, which had probably been made by former occupants. Through an open door leading to a living room Henry noted a TV with a huge screen. It looked expensive. The loud sobbing led to a bedroom on the right. He hated this part of his job. It seemed that increasingly he was forced to question people who were experiencing some sort of pain. After five years as a detective he should have developed a veneer, a callousness that would make it easier. But it hadn't happened. Each time was a new ordeal. When he saw the woman seated on the bed surrounded by several friends he knew this was going to be one of the worst.

She was short and heavy. Younger than he expected. Maybe thirty. She was wearing a long housecoat that had come open revealing a satin nightgown. She ran her fingers through her long, dark hair and it was a tangled mess. When her hands did stop moving, they clutched her face as though to hold back the sobs and tears. The women around her all came from the same mold. They looked up when Henry and Irene entered, their eyes hostile as though they blamed him for what had happened. Henry cleared his throat and began in his best Spanish.

"*Señora Sanchez. Estoy muy triste sobre...*uh." He was unable to remember words that would express his empathy. He looked at Irene.

"*Estamos muy tristed por su esposo,*" she said.

Mrs. Sanchez again ran the fingers of both hands through her hair, clutching it so hard it must have hurt. "*Por que?*" she moaned. "My Carlos never hurt nobody."

Henry did not believe she was aware that she was talking to a stranger. But that might be for the better. "Did you see who killed him?"

Her eyes rolled as though she could still see the killer. "It was a wild man. Loco."

"How do you mean?"

The woman looked up at him, her eyes veiled by tears. "He didn't have no clothes, just pants. *El pelo era muy largo. Malvado!*"

Irene interpreted. "His hair was very long. Malevolent."

"You think he was Cuban?"

She shook her head. "No, no! *Era Indio. Nativo. Malvado. Malvado!*"

"How big was he? Ah...*que grande?*"

The woman's hands waved, and her voice climbed, "*Grande! Grandisimo!*" For emphasis she came to her feet and thrust her arms above her head. "*Alto grandisimo!*"

Irene made a slight shake of her head. "She's exaggerating."

"I hope so."

Mrs. Sanchez gave a shrill screech of indignation. Then she erupted in a torrent of Spanish that Henry thought expressed her anger at all policemen and that a giant had killed her husband and cut off his head with a knife so big he had to hold it in both hands.

"*Señora,*" Henry interrupted. "Did your husband, *su esposa,* ever work in South America?"

She looked up at him, her fingers buried in her hair, her eyes swimming. "*Sud America? Si. Mucho veces. Bolivia, Columbia, Ecuador, mucho paises.*"

Henry looked at Irene. "I was afraid of that."

Irene turned to the woman. "*Señora. Su sposa,* did he ever work for

Trans-America Construction?"

"*Si, si,*" she answered and Henry felt a tingle of elation. This might be something he could use. Then she added, "Everybody work for Trans-Am."

Everybody? How many construction workers were there in Los Angeles? How many in California? The nation? He might as well try to establish a link between the killer and the entire construction industry. He looked at Irene. "Can you think of anything else to ask her?

Her expression was one of faint surprise as though she wondered if he truly was interested in her input. She shook her head. "No. Not at the moment."

She conveyed their regrets to *Señora* Sanchez who glared as though she held them responsible for the tragedy. The woman was shouting and pulling her hair when they walked out.

In the yard the two attendants from Gene Woods' office were loading the body into the coroner's ambulance. They climbed into the cab and drove away. The large bloodstain left in the dusty yard looked absurdly out of place. Gene Woods and Paul Rodriguez stood off to the side when Henry and Irene approached.

"What about it? Think it was the same guy who killed Trejo?"

"It's a possibility," Henry answered. "Sanchez worked in Ecuador. A laborer. Just like the guy who went to the consulate."

"You don't think that was Sanchez?"

"No. He doesn't fit the description."

"The man who did this," Irene said, "was the same man who killed the guard at the arboretum."

"You mean because of the curare. That is a strong connection."

"And they all had their heads removed, so there's another connection," Woods added. Then he grinned. "Or should I say *disconnection.*"

"He's got to be a psycho," Rodriguez said.

"I'm sure he is," Henry agreed. "But he's also an expert with that blowgun. And that makes him a very unusual psycho."

"I wonder what he did with the head?" Rodriguez nodded toward the trees. "I've got my guys looking for it."

Woods squinted at Henry. "You figure he might shrink it?"

Henry turned to Irene. "What do you think?"

She looked back at the house where the wailing of Mrs. Sanchez could still be heard. "Perhaps. If he knows how."

Despite his revulsion, Henry was also curious. He wondered how the head could be shrunk. In the jungle, the natives probably had some sort of secret herb that did the job. But the killer wouldn't find any head-shrinking herbs in L.A. Still, he'd found the vine to make curare. This was one smart Jivaro.

A young patrolman trotted toward them, holding his belt to keep its load of equipment from beating him to death. "Lieutenant," he called. "We found it."

Henry read the pallor in the patrolman's face. "Where?"

The patrolman pointed beyond the house. "Over there. Where he parked his car."

Woods snorted. "A headhunter with a car. It's got to be a Mercedes." Rodriquez lifted his chin. "What makes you think so?"

"All shrinks drive Mercedes," Woods said, and Rodriguez threw up his hands.

Henry turned to Irene. "Maybe you'd better take a look."

"That's why I'm here."

The patrolman led them along the edge of the trees to a side street. Several policemen were standing in knee-high dry grass and weeds near the curb talking in quiet tones and glancing down into the grass as though they didn't want to look, but could not resist. They moved aside and the patrolman pointed.

"There it is."

The skull of Sanchez was lying on its side, raw and bloody, the muscles and connective tissue exposed, bone glistening, the teeth bared in a bloody grin. The eyes bulged in a fixed stare of horror. The reflection of the low morning sun made them seem to glitter as though they still held life. The thin spike of a blowgun dart protruded from between the eyes. Henry glanced at Irene.

"You were right about him being a hell of a shot with that blowgun."

She was gazing at the skull, her mouth partially open. "I can't believe it. Only a Jivaro would do such a thing."

Gene Woods had seen hundreds of human skulls, but like the others, he stared, fascinated. "Why didn't he take the skull?"

Henry recalled his talks with Irene. "Didn't need it. Besides, the skull is heavy." He looked at her. "Right?"

Irene's eyes were amused. "You're learning."

Gene Woods knelt for a closer look. "Looks to me like that jaw has been broken a couple of times. Did this guy Sanchez have many fights?"

Paul Rodriguez had been talking to some of the patrolmen, and he turned to say, "Hell, yes. That guy didn't have one damn friend. I found about twenty people who said they're glad he's dead. You've got about a million suspects, Henry."

Henry nodded. "So what else is new?"

He stared down at the skull. Go ahead, grin. You know who did it, but you're never going to tell. And I don't know one damn thing I didn't know before. Instead, I have one more mystery: why did he kill this particular man?

CHAPTER 12

The shaman was pleased. He examined the *tsantsa* and told the warrior that he had done well to kill his enemy. Now the pain would go away and he would find peace. Except that the pain did not go away and it caused him to sweat as he strained to bear it the way a Jivaro warrior was supposed to bear pain. Maybe the pain was not going away because he had powerful enemies who were throwing darts into his head. That had to be the reason. There were other enemies he must kill. But who? Who were his enemies?

Steve wrenched himself awake, feeling suspended between reality and horror. With an effort he sat up, staring at the familiar outlines of his bedroom. The air felt cool on his sweaty body. Only the pain was still throbbing through his head and his body felt leaden, drained of energy.

Then he became aware that the pounding in his head was an echo of a pounding at his front door, the sharp sound echoing through the silent house. He glanced at his clock. Almost 5:00 o'clock. Shit. He'd lost the entire day. Who the hell could be coming to see him this late in the day?

When he got up, he was still wearing his pants. He stared down at them. Stains! What were those stains? Oh, God. His head tilted back in anguish. Not more blood!

The pounding at the door continued with the strident insistence of bad news. He put his hands over his ears. Aspirin. He had to have a couple of aspirin before he could answer the door.

He stumbled into the bathroom, pain lancing through his body. He was reaching for the medicine chest when he noticed that the sink was filled with pink-tinged water. Had he washed that from his hands? He pulled the plug and watched the water disappear taking with it his apprehension. Hell. He'd been dreaming. That was all.

He was passing the kitchen when he noticed heat coming from the open doorway. What the shit? Had he left the stove on all night? In this heat? What the hell was wrong with him? He entered the kitchen to shut off the gas and stopped in horror. There was a *tsantsa* hanging over the low flame of a burner on the stove. Oh, God! He knew that face! Even though the features were drawn into the tightly clinched look of a shrunken head with the lips and eyes sewn shut, he recognized Gordo Sanchez.

Oh, sweet Jesus! He really had gone hunting for Sanchez. This was impossible. He was losing his mind. The blood on his pants. The blood in the bathroom. It had to be from Sanchez. And, oh no! Those other times. Had he killed others? He couldn't have. But the head of Sanchez told a different story; something inside him was made of nightmares.

The pounding at the door was accompanied by a voice. "Steve! Steve!"

Helen? She must not see the *tsantsa*. She knew Sanchez. He turned off the fire and tore the head down. Where to hide it? There was a breadbox he never used in the corner of the sink and he thrust the *tsantsa* inside. The sink counter was a mess of pans, ball-bearings, and spilled rice and salt, but there wasn't much he could do about it now. He closed the kitchen door and strode to open the front door.

Helen gave a sharp gasp of relief. "Steve. I was so worried."

He held the door open for her. "Why? I'm okay."

She came inside and he closed the door. "I've been trying to call you all morning, but your phone is either off the hook or out of order." She walked into the bedroom and picked up the phone, which Steve saw had been knocked off its stand onto the floor. "You see. I thought something terrible had happened to you."

"Sorry about that. I guess I was restless last night."

"Last night? Steve, you haven't been to work for two days. What is going on?"

He didn't know and he was afraid to find out. Afraid to even think about it. To hide his fear, he turned away. "It's these damn headaches. I can hardly move."

The anguish in her voice said that her pain was as deep as his own. "Steve, I...you've got to see a doctor."

The thought of the *tsantsa* in the kitchen and the blood in the bathroom sent a chill through Steve. Which was worse? Having a doctor tell him he was going crazy, or living with the fear that he might kill again? And who would he kill next time?

"You're right." He picked up the address of Dr. Gutierrez from the top of the dresser. "This is the guy they told me about in Quito."

Helen glanced at the name. "I'll call him. We'll go right over."

"Without an appointment? No doctor—"

"He'll see you. He's got to." She picked up the telephone and dialed.

Steve glanced at his watch. "It's after five. He won't be in his office."

"I'll find him. You get ready."

She began dialing, but Steve didn't move. God, he didn't want to go. Then he pressed his fingers to his throbbing temples. What the hell was he doing? Why was he trying to evade the doctor when he knew it was his only hope?

He took a clean pair of pants and a white shirt from the dresser and went into the bathroom. He stripped off the stained pants and stuffed them into the clothes hamper along with his shorts. He pulled the shower curtains around the tub and turned the water on, letting it run for a few seconds to get as hot as he could stand it, hot enough to burn away the pain and the memories. He took the soap and lathered and scrubbed again and again, wishing he could reach that dirty blackness deep inside. But no amount of soap and water could take away either the darkness or the fear and he leaned his pain-filled forehead against the cool tiles.

The shower curtains slid aside and Helen reached in and touched him on the back. Steve almost fell. "Jesus! Don't do that," he yelped. She pulled her hand back and he felt a sense of loss. "On second thought, do it."

She parted the shower curtain and poked her head inside. She smiled mischievously, her eyes merry. "Need any help?"

The aspirin was working and he felt almost normal. "Sure," he said with a leer. "How about starting at the bottom and working your way up?" Her smile broadened and she touched her lips with the tip of her tongue. "I've heard that's the best way to get ahead."

She parted the shower curtains and Steve's pulse leaped. Her naked skin gleamed in the evening sunlight that filtered in through the small frosted window. She stepped into the tub and pulled the curtains closed with her hands behind her back. The water splashed off her face and hair, but she ignored it as she stood with her chin lifted, her lips parted. She looked like the alabaster statue of a goddess carved by a master. He was afraid to move, afraid that this moment too would turn into a dream.

She picked up the soap from the tray. "Turn around," she said. "Back first."

Instead, he put his arms around her and pulled her close. He kissed her with the warm water streaming over their faces and her smooth body feeling good under his hands. Breaking the kiss, he continued to hold her. "I love you, baby. I really do."

"I know," she said softly. "And I love you."

She kissed him again and Steve gave himself to the pleasure. For the first time in days he forgot the throbbing pain and the terrible dreams. His entire being was centered on this girl he loved and on the incredible sensation of her warm, tender hands and the beauty of the body that was all for him. With the warm water caressing them, they made love. Steve returned to reality with the shivering realization that cold water was cascading over them like winter rain.

"Oh, God," Helen said. "I'm freezing."

She climbed out of the shower in a rush of glistening legs and arms. Steve turned off the water before he followed. She was waiting with a huge fluffy towel that she wrapped around them and huddled close for warmth.

When they stopped shivering, she said, "I reached the doctor. He's going to be in his office at 6:30."

Steve hated the intrusion of the words. He wanted his life to stay exactly as it was at this instant, with Helen in his arms, her warmth making him forget the past and the future, the pain only a horror at the edge of his memory. He tightened his arms.

"Honey, I don't know what this doctor is going to say. But if I'm okay, or if he can make me okay, I want you to marry me."

She wrapped both arms around his neck and kissed him. The towel slid to the floor, but neither of them noticed.

They were both quiet as Helen drove along the Golden State Freeway toward downtown LA. Their love-making had created a sense of euphoria they both wanted to keep as long as possible. But the closer they came to their destination the more the sense of pleasure slipped away. By the time they arrived at the three-story medical center on Alvarado near Sunset Steve's headache had returned, and he tilted his head back against the head-rest and closed his eyes, willing the pain to go away. Helen's face was white with anxiety when she pulled to a stop in a parking lot next to the building.

The office of Dr. Gutierrez was on the top floor, his name stenciled on the glass of the door. Steve was slightly behind Helen, apprehension so strong he was almost sick. Helen reached for the doorknob and he touched her arm.

"Honey, would you mind if I go in alone?"

He wanted her to be by his side when the doctor told him what he knew would be bad news. But fear of what the doctor might reveal was an even greater dread. Suppose he was some kind of a monster whose dreams turned out to be horrible reality? No. He did not want Helen to hear what the doctor might have to say.

She started to protest, then smiled reassuringly. "Okay. There's a coffee shop next door. I'll wait for you there."

He smiled with a confidence he did not feel. "I won't be long."

"You'll be fine."

She kissed him on the cheek and walked toward the elevator, her back straight and her steps certain as though there really was nothing to worry about. But he knew it was a lie. She was almost as scared as he was. He opened the door and entered.

Dr. Gutierrez was waiting in the outer office near a four-drawer file cabinet and a receptionist's desk, an open folder in his hands. He was a short, thin man with dark hair that grew so low on his forehead that the tops of his glasses almost touched his hairline. He was wearing a dark suit complete with vest and necktie. He looked uncomfortable.

"Good afternoon. You are Steven Kelly?"

"That's right."

Dr. Gutierrez attempted a smile. "Well, I'm glad to see you." He motioned to a door. "Let's go into my office."

The office was large with three wide windows overlooking the roofs along Alvarado. The parquet floor was partially covered by an oriental carpet. An old wooden desk holding orderly stacks of files was situated so that light from the windows would come in from behind the expensive chair. Two hard wooden chairs waited in front of the desk. To Steve, they looked like seats in a gas chamber. A tall medicine cabinet was against one wall, the glass in the locked doors reinforced with imbedded wire mesh. Near it was a weight scale with a rod to measure height. A PC computer and printer were on a computer workstation near the desk.

Dr. Gutierrez placed the file folder on the desk. "Strip down to your shorts, please."

Steve did as he was told, hanging his clothing on a rack near the scale, feeling as though he was preparing for his own execution. The doctor began his examination.

As he took Steve's blood pressure, he said, "Dr. Hernandez wrote to me. I must say I expected you some time ago."

Steve stared at him. "You expected me?"

"Of course. The headaches must be very bad by now."

"Yes. That's why...wait a minute. How did you know about the headaches?"

Dr. Gutierrez gave him a puzzled look. "Do you have one now?"

"I always have one."

Gutierrez went to the medicine cabinet and unlocked it with a key he took from his pocket. He took a bottle of white tablets from the cabinet and broke a seal on the top.

"Take two every two hours, more often if you must." Steve pried the top off the bottle and shook two of the tablets into his palm and gulped them down. "Do you want water?"

"No, thanks." Steve hoped the pills would work fast. The headache was pounding through his head like a series of atomic explosions.

For fifteen minutes Dr. Gutierrez listened, prodded and peered, making notes on a standard examination form. Finally, he went behind his desk and told Steve to put his clothes back on.

As Steve was dressing, the doctor said, "Have the blackouts started?" Steve's fingers trembled so that he had trouble buttoning his shirt. "How did you know?" He knew the answer. Gutierrez had known all about him the instant he had told him his name.

"That's always the pattern with..." Gutierrez looked into Steve's eyes. "Dr. Hernandez did not tell you!"

Steve took a step toward him. "Tell me what, for God's sake?"

Gutierrez's face was filled with sorrow as he looked out the window. It was getting dark and the lights along Alvarado were coming on. "You've got to know," he said.

"Know what?" Steve barked, his body rigid. "What the shit is this?"

"Mr. Kelly, the jungle is full of many strange things."

What the hell was the man driving at? He was familiar with many of those 'strange' things. Like many heavy equipment operators he had worked in the jungles of Malaysia and the Amazon. But the worst had been the months in Ecuador. One time a guy on his crew was swimming in a jungle pool and accidentally cut his hand. The scent of blood brought the piranhas and before the man could scramble out of the water every ounce of flesh had been stripped from his body.

Another time he had seen a native girl bathing in a stream. Suddenly she screamed, not in pain but in fear, and she dashed out of the water screaming a name over and over. The other native women held her on the ground and spread her legs so they could peer into her vagina. One of them ran for the shaman who returned with a gourd of liquid, which he poured into the girl's vagina. In a moment a tiny fish flopped out and the girl stood up and sprang away from it in horror. One of the natives told Steve it was a *canero* fish. They swim into any orifice of a human or animal to lay their eggs, including a man's penis, and they can't be pulled out except with great pain because they have tiny quills like fishhooks. Sometime in the dim past a shaman had discovered that the juice of a certain plant would make them come out without a painful operation.

Yes. He knew enough to stay out of the rivers. If you didn't get killed by the piranhas or an electric eel or a *canero* fish didn't swim up your ass, the parasites would get you and starting eating your guts.

"So?" he said.

Gutierrez took a handkerchief from his pocket and dabbed at his lips as though he did not relish what he was about to say. "Have you ever heard of an amoeba parasite?"

"Wait a minute. Are you saying I picked up some kind of a bug, a microbe, while I was living with the Jivaros? Is that what this is all about?"

Gutierrez glanced down at the papers in the file folder. "The Jivaros? Ah, yes. The amnesia. You don't remember any of those three years?"

"Not consciously. But I have dreams."

Gutierrez hesitated. "Did you have such a...dream last night?"

"Yeah," Steve admitted. "It was like I was one of those natives, a Jivaro."

Gutierrez's face changed subtly as though a kernel of fear began to grow in his mind. His fingers drummed the file folder. "According to this report you have contracted such an amoeba parasite."

Relief flooded through Steve. A fuckin' microbe. He could handle that.

Gutierrez shook his head slightly. "It can be very serious."

Steve's fear returned like a slow tide. "How serious?"

Gutierrez pressed his palms together and beads of moisture formed on his forehead. "This particular parasite is generally contracted through swimming in contaminated water. Once inside the body it breeds copiously. It destroys the internal organs, making a particular attack on the brain."

Steve had to sit down. "Is that what's happening to me?"

"Dr. Hernandez ran many tests. There is no doubt. Your headaches and the blackouts confirm it."

Steve drew in a deep breath. Oh, Jesus God. How could this be happening? He was in the prime of his life, strong as a bull, with everything to live for.

"Can you help me?"

Gutierrez stared at him, his face drawn into deep lines. He slowly shook his head. "The only thing I can do is give you medication to help with the pain."

Steve stood up. He had to do something. He asked the one question whose answer he did not want to know.

"You're telling me I'm a dead man?" Steve felt as though a fist had been slammed in his stomach.

Gutierrez used a handkerchief to blot his forehead. "The headaches will get worse. So will the body pain, and the blackouts."

Steve ran his fingers through his hair. The fear was replaced by a numbing lethargy. He knew what Gutierrez was telling him was true, yet it was too incredible to be believed. It was almost as though they were discussing someone else. Except that the headaches were painfully real. And so were the blackouts. There was one more thing he had to know. One more answer he dreaded.

"Will I...could I go insane, before it ends?"

Gutierrez wet his lips. "It is inevitable. You could become very...violent."

Steve paced the floor. The headache was throbbing with a life of its own. When the shit was that medicine going to take effect?

"So what do I do? Just stand around and wait to die or go crazy? I can't do that. There's got to be something."

"If it had been caught early...perhaps." Gutierrez sighed. "But you were in the jungle three years. When Dr. Hernandez saw you it was already too late."

Steve stared at Gutierrez. "How much time do I have?"

Gutierrez raised his eyebrows. "You are young, very strong. It is hard to say.

Rage blazed through Steve and he reached across the desk and grabbed Gutierrez by the lapel of his jacket. "How long, Goddamn it? How long?"

"Months," Gutierrez yelped. "Many months."

The fear in Gutierrez's eyes burned away Steve's anger. Oh, shit. What was happening to him? He released Gutierrez and backed away. "I'm sorry," he said.

Gutierrez took a trembling breath, pity in his eyes. "I understand."

"That's a lie, isn't it?" Steve said, and Gutierrez shrank from the menace in his voice. "It isn't months, is it?" Gutierrez slowly shook his head. "How long?"

"Weeks. Maybe."

"Maybe?"

"All right. Maybe three. Four at the most."

Steve closed his eyes. It was over. Maybe it was best. If there was no cure for the pain, he would rather be dead.

Gutierrez watched him sadly. "When Dr. Hernandez informed me of your condition, I made arrangements for you at a...a place of security."

The throbbing in Steve's head exploded in a fiery burst of rage. "What the hell are you trying to say? You're putting me in an institution?"

Gutierrez pushed back his chair and stood up, his palms out. "No, no. Not an institution. It's a lovely place."

Steve walked around the desk. "That's why you ask about the dreams and what happened last night. You think I'm already crazy."

Gutierrez waved his hands, his eyes wide. "No, of course not. It's for your own happiness. You'll be taken care of. They can give you shots for the pain. They might even find a cure."

"Liar! That's a God damned lie!" The flame of pain was so bright it almost blinded him. Was every one his enemy? "You want to put me in a God damned jail!"

Gutierrez put his hands up, his face contorted in fear. "No, no. I won't tell them."

He knew! This man was an enemy. Worse. He was an evil shaman, a witch doctor of the blackest kind and he was planning to kill him. He had to stop him. He had only to put his hands around the evil shaman's neck and squeeze until the evil spirits went out of him and into the dream world where they would wait until another shaman could summon them to his bidding. When the shaman was limp under his fingers the pain began to go away. The shaman could no longer control the darts of the evil spirits.

As the pain subsided Steve found himself leaning on the edge of the desk. The body of Doctor Gutierrez was huddled in the corner as though he was curled up in sleep. What the hell was wrong with him? Why was he lying on the floor? He went to the doctor and shook him.

Then he saw Gutierrez's bloated face, his tongue protruding between his lips. On his neck were the vivid imprints of fingers. Steve looked around wildly, half expecting whoever had done this to spring at him. But he was alone. Alone? Oh, God. Another dream that was not a dream at all. He had killed this man. No wonder Gutierrez had wanted him locked up. He was already crazy. They would lock him up and throw away the key. He could not let that happen. Not when he was going to die. How long did he have? Weeks Gutierrez said. He couldn't spend them behind bars.

And yet, he might kill again. Nobody would be safe from him. He had to go some place where there were no people to kill. Where? Oh, Jesus. Where to go? The reservation! Of course. Back to the San Carlos. There in the silent woods he could hide where there would be no one for him to harm. He would start tomorrow. He had the pills the doctor gave him. They would keep him from going crazy with the pain until he was so deep in the forest it would not matter any more. Gutierrez would probably not be found until late tomorrow morning. By the time they tied him to the murder he would be long gone. By driving all night he could be in Arizona in the morning.

He was about to leave the office when he noticed his file folder on the doctor's desk. If the police found it they wouldn't give him a chance to reach the reservation. They would put him in prison and he couldn't allow that, not when he had such a short time to live. He folded the papers and stuffed them in his pocket and walked through the outer office, closing the door behind him, hearing the lock click. Wait. Fingerprints. His were all over the place. And the door was locked! What the hell? By the time he was identified he would be where they would never find him.

Outside the coffee shop he paused to review his story. He had to make Helen believe everything was okay. He had to look cheerful. Shit. If he pulled this off he should get the Academy Award. Thank God the pills Gutierrez had given him had taken most of the pain out of his headache. Inside he found Helen seated in a small booth with a cup of coffee in front of her, reading a newspaper.

"Hi, beautiful."

She hadn't seen him come in and his voice made her jump. When she quickly folded the paper and looked up, he was ready with a broad smile. She searched his face for a clue of what he had learned from the doctor.

Steve said, "Ready to go?"

"Sure." She dropped the folded paper on the seat and slid out of the booth.

"You forgot your paper."

"I'm finished with it," she said. She searched her purse for change to leave a tip and Steve noticed her hands trembling.

"I've got it." He placed a dollar on the table, then took her hands. "Hey, hey. Don't worry. The doctor said I'm going to be okay." He took the bottle of white tablets from his pocket. "See. He gave me these. They're all I need."

Some of the worry went out of her eyes. "Oh, Steve. I'm so glad."

Driving back to Sunland she was very quiet while Steve explained that the headaches were caused by a bug he had picked up in Ecuador and that the doctor suggested he take a brief vacation until the infection cleared up. "I thought I'd go home for a while," he concluded, keeping his voice light. "I've been meaning to go for a long time."

"Can you afford it?"

"I've got a little saved up. It won't take much. On the reservation I can live off the land."

"I mean, you told me a couple of weeks ago that Trans-Am owed you a lot of back pay." Her voice sounded fluttery around the edges as though she were treading carefully. "Did you ever collect it?"

"I tried to see the manager, but he wouldn't see me. When I got mad they threw me out. I never went back."

"Did the doctor say anything about…the dreams?"

Steve shot a quick look at Helen. She was staring ahead intently, her shoulders hunched as though she were expecting a blow, her hands tight on the steering wheel. He decided not to add to her worry.

"No. He's a medical doctor, not a psychiatrist."

"But he did say you'd be all right?"

Steve had to suppress a flash of anger. Why was she bugging him? He'd told her he was all right. He hated to keep repeating the same lie over and over. Maybe she sensed that he was holding something back. But there was no way he could tell her that he might turn into a raving maniac at any moment. What would be the point in making her afraid of him during the last few hours they would have together? And he didn't want her sympathy. That would be worse than the fear. So he grinned at her. "I'm okay. Believe me. All I need is a little rest."

But he had the impression that she didn't believe him, and during the remainder of the ride, she was silent.

When they arrived at his house his head began pounding again and he felt weak. He staggered when he got out of the car and Helen came to help him.

He straightened, saying, "I'm okay, baby."

"Are you sure?"

"Yeah. I'll take a couple more of those pills. They work pretty well." He opened the house door and held it for her, but she hesitated. "You're not coming in?"

"I shouldn't. I've got to get up awfully early, you know."

Steve felt a keen disappointment. "Hell, it's only eight o'clock. Come on. We can go out for dinner."

She looked into his face as though to read some message behind his eyes. "Okay. Maybe dinner. But that's all."

Before he changed his clothes Steve took two more of the white pills. He tried to estimate how much time he had before he had to begin the long drive. The cops wouldn't find Gutierrez until morning, so there was no danger there. He had the doctor's papers in his pocket so unless Gutierrez had told someone about the appointment, it might take weeks to tie him to his death. And nobody would connect him to the murder of Gordo Sanchez. There was no reason to hurry.

He froze at the sound of breaking glass. What the hell? The kitchen. Helen! She was in the kitchen. Oh, shit! He ran, dreading what he would find. At the open kitchen door, he stopped. Helen was standing in front of the sink staring at the open breadbox, a shattered glass at her feet. At that instant he felt hatred toward her so powerful it swept away all other feeling. She had betrayed him. She had seen the head of Sanchez and now his time was cut to nothing. He shoved past her and slammed the breadbox shut with a sound like an exploding shot.

"What the hell are you doing in here?"

Helen swiveled her unblinking eyes to him. "I…I came in for a glass of water."

"In the fuckin' breadbox?"

"I saw…I saw hair sticking out. I…" Her voice died to a whisper. "What is it?"

There was no point in denying it, was there? And she sure as hell hadn't recognized Sanchez. Maybe he was getting all excited about nothing. He opened the breadbox and took it out, holding it so that she couldn't get a clear look at the features.

"It's called a *tsantsa*, a shrunken head. I brought it back from Ecuador."

Helen backed away as though it would come to life. "Why? What on earth for?"

Steve faked a laugh. "Money. They're worth a couple of hundred bucks. Maybe more."

Helen shuddered. "Put it back. I don't want to look at it." She turned and went back into the living room.

Steve put the *tsantsa* back in the breadbox and followed Helen into the living room where she stood with her back to him. His head was throbbing again. He wished the damn pills would hurry up and take effect.

"I'm sorry, baby," he said. "I brought it back as a joke. I figured I'd show the guys at work. I'll get rid of it."

He put his arms around her and felt her stiffen so he moved back. What the hell was she so upset about? It was only a damn shrunken head.

She looked at him, her lips trembling in a tense smile. "Maybe I'd better go."

"What about dinner?"

She moved toward the door. "Can I take a rain check until you get back?" She reached up to touch his cheek. "I know you're not feeling well. I think it would be better if we waited. Don't you?"

Waited? It would be a long wait. But maybe it was better this way. He would have a hell of a time putting up a cheerful front through a long dinner. He might let something slip and ruin everything. It would be better if she remembered him the way he used to be.

"Maybe you're right. We'll have plenty of time when I get back."

She pressed her lips together, then with effort smiled. She put her arms around his neck and kissed him. She pulled away and put her head against his shoulder with her arms around him.

"Steve, I'm sorry," she whispered. "I'm so sorry."

He brushed his hand over her hair. He loved the feel of its silken texture, its smell of sunlight. It was hard to believe that this would be the last time he would ever touch her, would ever hold her close.

His voice was husky when he said, "It's all right, baby. Just remember, I love you. I always will."

"I'll remember."

She kissed him again on the cheek and turned away. When she walked down the steps to her car she was crying, and he was struck by the uneasy feeling that she knew everything. What other reason could there be for her strange behavior? She'd acted as though she was afraid of him. But why? If she suspected that he was lying, that he might even be dying, that shouldn't make her afraid of him. Unless she thought that what he had was contagious. Except it wasn't that kind of fear. She acted like he was going to turn into some kind of monster and kill her. He caught his breath. Just like he had killed Gutierrez.

Could that be it? She'd started acting strange the minute they'd left the doctor's office. But she couldn't know about Gutierrez. And there was no way she could have found out about Sanchez. The newspaper! Shit! She'd been reading the newspaper when he came into the coffee shop, and she'd put it down awfully damn fast. Folded it up even. There had to have been a story about the murder. And she knew how he felt about Sanchez.

He went into the house and closed the door. He leaned back against the door, thinking. Would she call the police? Not the way she felt about him. He looked at his watch: 7:30. He would throw a few essentials in his car then grab a couple hours of sleep before the long drive to Arizona. A couple of hours delay wouldn't hurt anything. The white pills he'd taken would hold his headache at bay for at least two hours. By the time the pain returned he'd be on his way. Once on the reservation, he'd be okay. Hell.

He might even beat this thing.

He was feeling almost like his old self when he drifted off to sleep thinking about Helen. He was glad he'd ask her to marry him. He should have done it a long time ago. They were right for each other. They would have a wonderful life together, a life that would last forever.

CHAPTER 13

Henry Warner decided that this moment would forever be his benchmark of happiness. It was a moment of memories, of satin and velvet, rich with brocaded reds and golds. After this night it did not matter if everything else was all downhill. He was with one of the most beautiful women he'd ever seen; they were seated in a booth in his favorite restaurant, which was almost deserted; Oscar, at the piano in the corner, was playing and crooning a haunting love song. Best of all was a euphoria that made him feel like a born-again teenager. And it was all because he suspected that Irene Perez liked him, maybe even liked him a lot.

Perhaps it was his imagination, but she seemed to enjoy being with him as much as he enjoyed her company. She had certainly gone out of her way to look her most gorgeous. It had to be for him. She was wearing a strapless evening gown of dark green crushed velvet that was stunning in its simplicity. A single strand of pears set off her flawless skin. She had loosened her hair and it cascaded in dark ringlets that highlighted her delicate, but strong features. She had done some invisible thing to her eyes that made them incredibly luminous, and so magnetic that looking at them drew him into a world so warm and exotic there was no escape.

Henry hoped that the dark suit he'd bought for the occasion was doing its job. If clothes made the man he should be on solid ground. The suit, shirt, tie, and shoes had taken almost his entire paycheck, and he'd shaved so close that his skin hurt. Was this what it was like to be in love; to care so much for someone that you went overboard to please them; reveling in the knowledge that you would soon be with her, and at the same time, feeling a morbid depression at the slightest nick of the razor, the slightest hair out of place? How could such pleasure and such misery exist simultaneously?

But the apprehension was over. They were together, and she was sitting closer than she had to, looking at him when she didn't have to, and hardly touching her food. He would have been content to remain silent laved by the exhilaration, but he was afraid she would think him a bore, so he rolled out some scintillating conversation.

"In Ecuador, I understand you're a teacher—a professor."

She was slow in answering as though she, too, did not want to break the mood. "Yes. At the university in Quito."

Henry took her left hand and studied her delicate fingers. Except for the pearl necklace and pendant earrings, she wore only one other piece of jewelry: a brilliant sapphire on the ring finger of her right hand.

"I never did ask you," he said. "Are you married?"

She smiled. "No."

Henry let his breath out slowly. That had been a strain on his heart. He should have checked on her marital status sooner. He could have ruined his psyche. Irene turned her hand over to take his, and he couldn't believe the pleasure that coursed through his body. She look up at him and raised an eyebrow. *ed*

"No," Henry said hastily. "So far, no takers."

Her fingers were warm and gentle. She touched his palm with her other hand and he felt as though she had touched his heart. "Hm. Too bad." His disappointment was so strong he felt his skin chill. She wanted him to be married? Then she added, "for them," and his heart leaped.

This was foolish. In less than one second, he had roller-coasted from delight to pain and back to delight, and all because of this woman's voice. She probably thought he was only one cut above an idiot. She had to be used to men with more control, more *savoir-faire*. He would have to watch himself, use some mental discipline. But even as he was making the resolution he heard his voice sounding like a simpering fool.

"Oh? What makes you say that?"

"Your hands. They're a giveaway."

"Oh, oh. From now on gloves."

Brilliant repartee. About as scintillating as a computerized robot. But she was laughing!

"No, no. They're nice. They tell me good things."

What the hell? Go with the flow. He took one of her hands and studied it, touching her palm, hoping it would produce the same sensation in her as her touch had for him.

"Hm. Wicked. I see a trail of men with broken hearts." She giggled and he touched her palm to his lips. "But they thought it was worth it." God, he was corny.

"A very short trail, I'm afraid."

Henry continued to hold her hand. "And now?"

"No one special."

Henry grinned at her and she cocked her head. There had been a few women in his life from time to time, but no one special, certainly no one special at the moment, thank heavens. Maybe his attraction toward this woman was because he had reached a point in his life when he was psychologically ready for marriage. He had read somewhere that men— and probably women—tend to get married when they were susceptible to the idea. Generally, they married the person they happened to be going with at the time; or rather, the person who most closely met their criteria. When you started looking at women and wondering how well they would wear over the years, it was time to back away. Except that with this woman he wanted to be vulnerable. Didn't he? He sure as hell did at the moment. Tomorrow could take care of itself.

As though reading his mind, Irene said, "What is the plan for tomorrow?"

What was she talking about? Oh, yes, the Trejo killing. Jesus. She'd made him forget all about the case. He really was getting in over his head. He released her hand and sat back, sipping his coffee.

"I've got people checking on this Sanchez. So far all we know is that he was a construction worker, truck driver, and equipment operator."

"The same as the man who went to the office of *Señor* Trejo."

"Yes. But Sanchez doesn't fit the description. We're checking with the people where he's working now, but we haven't found out much. Nobody liked him. He's had fights with everybody."

"His wife said he'd worked in Ecuador."

"We'll start checking with the State Department tomorrow. See if we can get a line on any construction workers who recently came back from Ecuador."

"Won't that take an awfully long time?"

Henry took her hand again. "I hope so," he said, and, when she smiled, he almost hoped the killer would never be caught so that she would stay forever.

Irene toyed with her knife. "I hope this won't sound foolish."

"Foolish?" Henry could not conceive of her ever sounding foolish. "Why should it?"

"Well, I was thinking. Perhaps the person we're searching for became ill in Ecuador."

"I suppose. He might have come here to see a doctor, you mean?"

"Yes. And if he is a native of Ecuador, don't you think he might try to see a doctor also from there? Certainly one who speaks Spanish."

Henry looked at her with a swell of pride. By God, she was as brilliant as she was beautiful. "You're right. I'll get someone checking on the doctors from South America. Only, again, it's going to take time. There's got to be hundreds."

"Start with the ones from Ecuador. There can't be many."

"I'll see if we can identify them. Somebody should know." He grinned at her. "Are you sure you're not a detective at home."

She looked at him from the corners of her eyes. "Maybe I will stay here. Get your job."

"I'll get you on the force. We can be partners."

Her eyes captured his. "That would be even better."

She lowered her eyes, but the color deepened in her cheeks and his pulse quickened. He should be so lucky.

In the hot bedroom of his home in Sunland Steve Kelly stirred, his arms and legs tensing as another dream clawed images from his memory. He was a Jivaro warrior and he was walking through the jungle with his blowgun looking for game. Suddenly he saw a strange tree trunk and he wondered what it was. As he watched the tree changed into a beautiful Jivaro woman who looked at him. He smiled and started toward her. Then her face changed into an evil mask and she screamed and pointed at him. She came toward him darts pouring from her mouth and flashing between them to sink into his head, setting his brain on fire. He clutched his head in agony and the woman laughed and her face became young and beautiful, and her hair blonde. It was the blonde woman and she wanted to kill him.

The warrior's eyes snapped open. They felt raw and out of focus.

His body was pain-wracked, covered with sweat. There was something he was supposed to do. Something about an enemy who was trying to kill him, throwing darts into his brain. It was the blonde woman. She must be very powerful to be able to throw darts. Or maybe she was not a woman at all. Maybe she was an evil spirit who had taken the form of a woman. But spirit or not the woman was an enemy. She knew about the other enemies he had killed. She knew about the man called Sanchez. She might even suspect about the man called Gutierrez. She might tell the police and they would put him in prison. She must be killed. And he knew where to find her.

He got up and put on the pants, shirt, and shoes he had grown used to wearing. He found his blowgun and darts in the building called the garage and he hung the pouch of darts on his belt. There was also a long knife that he put in his belt. Then he went to the machine and drove away.

When he came to the place where the woman lived he left the machine where it would not be easily seen. Taking the blowgun he walked up the gentle slope of hill behind the building until he was opposite a balcony with a large window that opened into the largest of the woman's rooms. The night was warm and the window was open with the gossamer curtains pulled aside so that he could see into the lighted room. Good, she had not gone to bed. He squatted in the bushes and tried to ignore the pain that radiated throughout his body.

The woman came through a doorway into the room and he tensed. She was wearing a short gown that was made for sleeping, but she did not appear to be ready for sleep. She walked about the room smoothing her long hair with her hands. Once she stopped in front of a telephone-thing and stared at it and he stood up. For some reason the telephone-thing meant danger for him. His eyes narrowed into slits. She was talking on the telephone-thing. He could hear her clearly.

"Hello. Is this the police? Yes. I—" Quickly he swung the blowgun into position and inserted a dart. Then she said, "No. Cancel that," and placed the telephone down.

He relaxed. Maybe she was not an enemy after all. She picked up the telephone again and began punching its buttons. He lifted the blowgun. But she did not talk. Instead, she listened for a few second.

"Oh, Steve, Steve. Please answer," she muttered.

Steve? Why was that name familiar? The woman replaced the telephone and began pacing the floor.

"Oh, Steve. Where are you?"

Steve? He stood up as memory fought through the pain. He was Steve. She was trying to call him. But he was here. What the hell was he doing standing outside Helen's apartment? Oh God! Another blackout. Another nightmare. The last he could remember was packing his car for the trip and going to bed. He had no memory of driving here. Why had he come? Maybe Helen had said she would come with him. The thought made him feel better. That had to be it. But what was he doing with the blowgun?

He went back to his car and put the blowgun, darts, and knife in the trunk. There was a disquieting comfort in knowing they were there. Besides, they wouldn't matter as long as he could keep the blackouts at bay. Now, sleep was his enemy. He had to be sure he didn't go to sleep. He found the white pills he'd put in the glove compartment and gulped down two more. He looked at the few remaining with dismay. They were going awfully fast. Even so, if he took it easy they should last until he got to the reservation. Right now he had to talk to Helen. He combed his hair as he climbed the steps to her apartment door, and rang the bell.

After a moment she asked, "Yes? Who is it?"

"Steve," he said, and he heard her intake of breath, then the locks were released and she was in his arms. "Oh, Steve. I was so worried. I tried to call you."

Steve drew strength from the feel of her strong, supple body under his hands. "I'm sorry. I should have called. But I...I had to see you."

She searched his face with a mixture of anxiety and fear. "Are you all right?"

The headache had diminished and he was able to dredge up a chuckle. "Sure." He moved away from her, trying to find words that would allay her suspicions. "But I didn't tell you everything the doctor said. He told me that I'm going to feel pretty bad for a while. I'm really going to need that rest. But it's a long drive. I'm...I'm not sure I can make it alone."

Helen closed the door, taking her time before she turned back to him. "You want me to come with you?"

"Only as far as the reservation. You can bring my car back."

"But you'll need it."

Steve's smile was grim. "Not for a long time, I'm afraid."

She came to him and put her arms around him. He had the feeling that she knew he would not be coming back—ever. But she also knew about Sanchez and he could feel the trembling of her body as she tried to decide what to do. He had to make her believe him. Without her, he could never keep the nightmares away. And the nightmares meant that someone would die. What was more important, keeping his pride or committing murder?

"Honey," he said, "I hate to ask you. You know me. I never ask for help from anybody. But I don't think I can make it. I need you. I can't do it alone."

He felt her muscles relax. "All right. I'll do it."

He held her closer, realizing just how much she must love him. And he struggled to bury an evil thought in a dark corner of his mind—now she would not be able to call the police.

CHAPTER 14

As Henry Warner studied the tear-streaked face of the nurse, he had a painful sensation of *deja vu*. Twice in the last few days he'd seen similar faces: Latin women weeping for their dead. He avoided the distasteful task of breaking in on her grief by looking around the reception room. Not much to see. Typical for the area. A receptionist's desk, sliding window between the reception room, and the waiting room, a couple of four-drawer filing cabinets, thin wall-to-wall carpeting, a couple of nondescript silk-screen prints on the wall. And, now, a room filled with the sound of a weeping woman. The room didn't tell him a thing, so he turned to the woman.

"I know you've talked to the other detectives, *Señora* Granados, but I've been working on another case that might help us find out who killed Dr. Gutierrez. Do you think you might be able to answer two or three questions?"

"I don't know," she sniffed.

Señora Granados was a short woman of forty or so with a big stomach and shoulder-length dark hair shot with gray. She was wearing a white nurse's uniform and one or more rings on each finger. Her high cheekbones and low forehead reminded Henry of pictures he had seen of Aztec or Inca Indians. She had discovered the body of Dr. Gutierrez when she came in at nine o'clock and had called the police. Detectives Hertoc and Adams had called Henry as soon as they found out that Gutierrez was from Ecuador. The call had surprised Henry. He had only put out the word a half-hour before to call him if anything came in involving a South American doctor, particularly a doctor from Ecuador. He'd immediately called Irene and she'd come with him. Now she was standing next to *Señora* Granados with a sympathetic hand on her shoulder.

"Please. You can help us to catch his man."

The woman drew in a shuddering breath. "I will try."

Broc Adams, a big-shouldered black man who had recently been promoted to detective sergeant, said, "Louie and I tried to question her, but we couldn't get much."

"Okay. Thanks, Broc." He turned back to *Señora* Granados, offering his handkerchief.

She took it, and murmured, "*Gracias.*" She choked back a deep sob. "*Por que? El era tan bueno. Por que alguin quiere matarlo?*"

"I'm sorry. No *hablo Espanol.*"

Once again, Henry told himself he was going to take Spanish lessons. Maybe Irene would give him lessons. Thank God he was a slow learner. He looked at Irene and made a nod toward the woman, signaling her to see what she could do. Irene put her head close to the older woman's and consoled her in Spanish, her voice low and sympathetic.

"*Habla Usted English, Señora?*"

Señora Granados nodded. "*Si.* We have many *pacientes Americanos.*"

Henry knelt beside the nurse. "*Señora*, perhaps you can help us find the man who did this terrible thing."

Señora Granados looked at Henry as though seeing him for the first time. "*Si,*" she stammered. "I will try."

Henry took out his pad and pen. "Did Dr. Gutierrez have any appointments last night?"

"No, no. He go before I go. I lock the *officina* as always."

"That means he came back for some reason. Would it be possible for someone to call him at home and make an appointment?"

She wiped her nose with the handkerchief. "We have answering service. In emergency, they will call."

Henry looked at Broc Adams. "You might check that out." Adams nodded and went into the doctor's office were Louie Hertoc was directing the lab crew. "Now, *Señora*, this is very important. Did Dr. Gutierrez have any patients who were natives of the Montaña region of Ecuador?"

Señora Granados looked at him, her brimming eyes puzzled. "We have many patients from Ecuador."

"But did you have any from the jungles?"

"La Montaña." Irene interjected.

"La Montaña? Perhaps. *Quien sabe?*"

Henry looked at Irene. "Can you get anything more definite?"

She pulled a chair up and sat beside the nurse. "Did you have any *de esos Indios pacientes?* Jivaros?"

The woman's eyes opened wide. "*Indios?* Oh, no, no. *Nunca, nunca.*"

"Are you sure?" Henry asked.

"*Si.* I am sure." She blew her nose into Henry's handkerchief and he winced.

Irene said to him, "I still can't believe it could be a native."

"If it isn't, we've got about a million suspects."

Irene thought a moment. "Maybe not. There are many doctors in Los Angeles from Ecuador. If this was the same man we are searching for he must have had a reason to call Dr. Gutierrez. And how did he know he was from Ecuador?"

"Maybe he just got lucky."

"It is more likely, don't you think, that he knew this doctor, or knew about him."

Henry felt a spark of hope. Maybe she'd hit upon something that could give them a lead. Then he shook his head. "That may be. But it's more likely that he heard about him from a friend, anybody."

"But suppose that person was in Ecuador, perhaps even Quito."

"Meaning he got the doctor's name while he was in Ecuador."

"*Verdad.* Let us assume that this person, who is not a native but is very familiar with the Jivaro, is only recently from the Montañas. It is possible that if he is suffering from an illness, it might have begun there. Perhaps that is why he left the country."

Her point snapped into place and Henry was disgusted with himself for not thinking of it and proud of Irene because she had. She must think him a real *estupido.* "So he could have been in a hospital there. And if he was, his doctor might have told him to contact Gutierrez when he got back here."

"When he came home."

"Of course." Henry resisted an urge to hug her. "He's from LA. Wait a minute. Maybe he just came to LA for treatment. A lot of people do that."

"Then why wouldn't *Señora* Granados know about him? And why would he have to make an emergency appointment?"

"You're right again. We know he didn't just arrive."

He couldn't take his eyes from Irene. Her slightly almond eyes had grown round and her cheeks had changed from pale bronze to delicate pink. She was like a fox closing in for a kill. He hated to bring her back to reality.

"There are hundreds of hospitals in Ecuador," he said. "We're never going to get a line on him that way. It'll take weeks."

"No. The only hospital near the Montaña where they would bring a foreigner is in Quito." She turned to *Señora* Granados who had been sobbing so that Henry's handkerchief was now also sodden. "Have you had any *correspondencia* with the hospital in Quito?"

The woman tried to focus through spilling tears. "*Correspondencia?*"

"The hospital," Irene repeated. "Did Dr. Gutierrez know any doctors in Quito?"

Señora Granados's face cleared. "Oh, *si.* Dr. Hernandez."

Irene shot Henry a look of satisfaction. "Have you had any *correspondencia* with Dr. Hernandez recently? A letter? Telephone calls?"

"Oh, *si.* Many *cartas*—letters."

Henry could wait no longer. "Do you have them here?"

She looked at a large filing cabinet. "*Si,* I have them."

"Would you get them please?"

She got to her feet as though her body was fighting gravity and walked to the filing cabinet. She opened a drawer and leafed through the contents. Henry hovered over her shoulder. Irene came to stand beside him and he could almost feel her body quiver with anticipation.

Behind them Broc Adams said, "I checked with the answering service. They put through the call all right. But they didn't get a name."

"Okay," Henry said, without turning. "We might have something here."

Señora Granados fumbled a folder from the file and handed it to Henry. "*Aqui.* These are the letters from Dr. Hernandez. *Todos.*"

Henry snatched the folder from her and carried it to the reception desk where he sorted through its contents. There were perhaps a dozen letters bearing the letterhead of the Quito hospital, but all were written in Spanish. He looked at Irene who was pressed against him as she peered at the letters.

"I guess you're going to have to do this."

"Of course," she said. "I'm glad to help."

When she sat at the desk and scanned the letters her eyes danced with excitement, thoroughly enjoying the puzzle. He hoped she would not get the thrill of the hunt in her blood the way he had. If she did, ordinary life would never be the same. On the other hand, he thought as he stood admiring the nape of her neck, if she enjoyed it enough she might not return to Ecuador. Maybe he could get her listed as a permanent consultant to the LAPD. She made a soft cry and his thoughts came back into focus. She straightened, holding one of the letters. "Here. In this one he is telling Dr. Gutierrez about a patient who had been living with the Jivaros."

Broc Adams said, "Does he have a name?"

She looked up at Henry in triumph. "Steve Kelly. He was a construction worker."

Henry felt the same sense of satisfaction he always got at that instant when the pieces fell into place. "Steven Kelly. Try the unions."

"Got it." Adams crossed into the other office and they heard him pick up the phone.

Henry motioned to the letter. "What else is there?"

Irene was scanning the letter. "Kelly was picked up in the jungle. He was suffering from amnesia. Dr. Hernandez thinks he'd been living with the Jivaros!"

"Was he from LA; does it say?"

"Yes, yes." Her voice was charged with excitement. "He'd been working on a construction project building a road when they were attacked by Jivaros. That's the last he remembered until he woke up in the hospital...three years later!" She looked up at Henry, her eyes glowing. "He lived with the Jivaros for three years."

"And if he had amnesia he wouldn't remember anything about his past."

"He probably thought he was a Jivaro."

Henry remembered the fleshless skull of Gordo Sanchez grinning in the grass. "Evidently he still does. But why? Any clue in there?"

Irene scanned the paper. When she spoke there was a new tone in her voice, a sadness that made Henry glance from the letter to her face.

"The reason Dr. Hernandez is telling all this to Dr. Gutierrez is because he asked Steven Kelly to see Dr. Gutierrez when he got back to Los Angeles."

"To treat the amnesia?"

"No. Kelly picked up a parasitic infection in the jungle. He called it," she glanced at the letter, "Cringescua Allandida. It's a parasite that attacks the nervous system, generally the brain. The victim goes mad. They usually die within a few months."

"So that's it." Henry walked to the window and looked down at the cars moving in the heat radiating from Alvarado Street. "The poor bastard is going crazy. He probably doesn't even know what he's doing."

"He must think he's still a Jivaro."

Señora Granados stopped sobbing, muttered, "Mio Dio," and crossed herself.

Henry turned away from the window. "He probably slips in and out of it or he wouldn't be able to function at all."

Irene put the letter down. "I wonder why he didn't take the head of Dr. Gutierrez?"

"Either he was interrupted, which doesn't seem likely since nobody called us, or maybe he killed him when he wasn't a headhunter. And if it did happen that way, he's probably scared as hell. He might be running right now. Excuse me."

The inner office was a scene of controlled chaos. The police photographer circled the body of Dr. Gutierrez snapping pictures. A fingerprint team was dusting every article that looked as though it might have the remotest connection with the crime. Gene Woods was watching Louie Hertoc, who looked more like a bearded psychology student than a detective as he taped an outline of the body on the floor. Broc Adams was sitting on the edge of the doctor's desk using the telephone. Both the desk and the telephone were sprinkled with dusting powder, as were Adam's pants.

Henry wished he could hear the other end of Broc Adams conversation as the big detective listened to a voice on the telephone and made notes. He glanced at Adams' note pad, then caught himself. He was becoming impatient and that disturbed him. The job had enough occupational stress without adding to it. Beside, the appearance of impatience might ruin his stolid, laid-back image. Still, he was relieved when Adams ended his phone conversation.

"Okay. Thanks. I'll stop in later and check the file if it's okay. Yeah. Thanks."

Adams hung up the phone and picked up his note pad. "Steven Kelly. Heavy equipment operator. Six-one, one-ninety. Black hair, brown eyes. Caucasian. Half Apache Indian. And get this: he just came back from South America."

Henry stared at him. "What was that about an Indian?"

"Half Apache. Don't ask which half."

Henry didn't smile. "That might explain a few thing. Did they have an address?"

"No, but he's working for Grady Construction in Eagle Rock; 1103 Oak."

Henry wrote it down. "Get an APB out on this, code 918-V."

Gene Woods took a step toward them. "Violently insane? You sure about that?"

"He's the headhunter. What do you think?"

Woods nodded. "I wouldn't argue."

"I'm going out to Eagle Rock," Henry said. "Have a couple of units meet me there with a warrant. But tell them not to take any action unless the suspect tries to flee. Okay?"

"Got it." Adams picked up the phone.

Henry hurried into the outer office. "Irene," he began. "Dr. Perez. We've got his work address. I'm going out there. Either Adams or Hertoc'll see that you get to your hotel."

Irene grabbed her purse off the desk. "I'm going with you."

Henry put up his hand. "No. This could be dangerous."

Her chin lifted and her jaw tightened. "Suppose he's gone back to being a Jivaro?"

"That's even worse. I don't want you hurt."

"You want to kill him." Her voice was flat, accusing.

Henry felt a surge of anger. "Of course not. We don't set out to kill anybody."

"Then you'll need me."

She was right. He hadn't been lying when he said he didn't want to kill the man. And if he had reverted, he might not even speak English.

Damn.

"Okay," he agreed, and he saw a flash of triumph in her eyes. "But you do exactly as I tell you. Okay?"

"Yes, I am at your orders."

She smiled, and Henry knew that if she had smiled like that when she'd asked if she could go, he wouldn't have been able to say no. He must remember that and start building his defenses or he could be in big trouble.

He stood aside so she could lead the way out the door. As he followed Henry wasn't thinking about the job; he was thinking of the last thing she had said and wishing she would say it to him again when this whole mess was over.

By using the siren Henry made it to the Oak Street address in fifteen minutes. It turned out to be the construction site of what would be a huge apartment or condominium complex. He cut the siren before he got too close, then swung into a dusty parking area near a trailer home. A sign on its side identified the GRADY CONSTRUCTION CO. There was a black-and-white parked on the street. Henry showed the two officers his badge and told them to keep out of sight. He would let them know if their man was at the site.

Walking with Irene to the trailer Henry checked the work going on. The construction was in its early stages and heavy equipment was being used to dig a deep hole that would be the foundation or an underground garage. He wondered if one of the men operating the machines with such precision could be his killer. If he was he certainly wasn't exhibiting any sign of insanity. Even so, if he was here and he suspected trouble, he could be dangerous. Maybe he should ask Irene to wait in the car. But she was already well ahead of him, opening the door to the small trailer home. Henry grinned and shook his head. She was like a rookie detective about to make her first big bust.

When he entered the trailer she was standing at a counter littered with blueprints and a stocky man with red hair and wearing a shirt with no necktie was approaching, his eyes taking in Irene with appreciation.

He smiled, and said, "Hello, there. What can I do for you?"

Henry answered, "Are you Grady?"

The man's eyes jumped to him. Henry understood that. Irene had that effect on men.

"Who's asking?" Both his eyes and his voice had assumed a chill.

Henry showed him his badge and identified himself, and tried to warm the air with a smile. "Sorry to disturb you, but I need a little information about one of your employees."

Grady's voice did not thaw. "The lady was first." He turned to Irene and his smile returned.

Irene smiled back. "We're together."

To his credit Grady kept his smile, but it lost a step. "Oh. Yeah, I'm Grady. Who're you looking for?"

"Steven Kelly. You know him?"

Grady's smile slid away and his forehead wrinkled. "Steve? Why do you want him?

"We just want to ask him a few questions. Is he here?"

Grady shook his head. "Hasn't been here for two days. Three, counting today."

"How was he then? Did he act, uh, normal? His usual self?"

Grady rubbed his chin. "Not really. He gets these headaches. Seems like he's in a daze about half the time."

Irene said, "That's it."

"What is it?" Grady said. "He's okay, isn't he?"

Henry looked away. It was hard to look someone in the eye when you had bad news. And the man obviously cared about what happened to Kelly.

"We won't know that until we find him."

"We want to help him," Irene added.

Grady ran his blunt fingers through his thinning red hair. "Jesus, I hope so. I like Steve. Everybody does."

"Do you have an address for him?"

"Yes, but he won't be there. Helen's driving him back to the reservation."

Henry stiffened, a tiny alarm building. "The reservation?"

"Sure. Didn't you know? He's Apache."

Irene nodded. "That's why he could survive with the Jivaros."

"Which one? Which reservation?"

"One of those in Arizona. Helen told me when she called. It's near Phoenix—a Spanish name. San Carlos; that's it." He looked at his watch.

"They should be there soon."

Hell, now he had to go charging off to some Indian reservation in the middle of nowhere. "Who is this Helen?"

"She works here. She and Kelly go together. I figured they were going to get married." Grady's voice took on a note of fear. "She isn't in any trouble, is she?"

Was she? Kelly had killed four people. Would she be next? He looked at Irene.

"I don't think so," she said to Grady, "unless he thinks she's an enemy."

"An enemy? He'd never think of Helen that way."

"I hope to hell not," Henry said. "May I use your phone?"

Grady lifted a lid on the counter so that Henry could pass through. Henry turned to Irene. "I'm going to call the Arizona Highway Patrol. And the reservation police."

"The reservation police?"

"They police the reservations. If he's there, we'll need their support."
"It is jungle, this reservation?"

"Sort of. Forests, I think."

"I hope they find him before he gets there. If he is a real Jivaro, you will never catch him."

Henry was thinking about that as he reached for the telephone. According to that paper in Dr. Gutierrez's office the guy only had a few more weeks to live, maybe a few days. Starting a manhunt might endanger a lot of lives and he sure as hell wouldn't want to go chasing through the woods after the crazy bastard. Wouldn't it be better to simply let him die?

Then he realized he couldn't do that. It was the duty of law enforcement to bring in the killer, not to be judge, jury, and executioner. Besides, the killer had a girl with him who might be a hostage, a girl whose life might be in extreme danger. They had to find Kelly—and fast.

CHAPTER 15

The long drive had been agony for Steve. By taking the white pills every couple of hours he managed to suppress the pain enough to drive as far as Phoenix before fatigue forced him to turn the driving over to Helen. But the mental anguish of what he might do if he blacked out was a greater agony than the throbbing pain in his head. He had to make plans while he still had the ability to reason.

He leaned back against the headrest and went over his timetable for the thousandth time. When would Gutierrez be discovered? Not until the nurse came in. That would be 8:00 at the earliest. By the time the police arrived it would be about 8:30. Even if they were to find something he'd overlooked that would lead to him—fingerprints probably—it would take time to process the information. No. There was no way they could learn where he was for hours, maybe days, as long as he had the blonde so she could not betray him. The woman! Steve's head snapped up and Helen gave him a startled glance.

"Are you all right?"

"Yes, sure," he said.

But was he? Jesus Christ! He'd been thinking of her as a woman, not as Helen; a woman who would betray him. He had to maintain control. He must keep alert. If he went to sleep the blackouts would come. That was when the dreams came. And the dreams brought death. He looked out the window, studying the terrain. That's it. Think of where you were and what you were going to do when you got to the San Carlos.

"That little town we just passed was Seneca. We'll be crossing the Salt River pretty soon. We're almost there."

"Okay." She stared intently at the road, which now wound through mountainous terrain and thick stands of evergreens. "What happens then?"

"I'm going to head inland, west; over toward Canyon Creek. It's wild as hell in there." He smiled, keeping his voice light as he lied. "There's a native doctor I know about there. I'll check in with him. Maybe I can get in touch with my gods."

He thought about what he had said. Was that what he was after—to get in touch with his Apache gods? Could they...would they help? He'd always wondered in a vague way what it would be like to be dead. Would he float down the Colorado River in a hollow log to reach the place where the spirits lived? Or would he meet Big Owl, the cannibal god who would strip his flesh from his bones? Was that better than meeting Gain, the supernatural God of the underworld? Maybe they would throw spirit darts into his skull the way his enemies did. Hadn't his mother told him about an Apache god called 'Killer-of-enemies'? Maybe the Jivaros and the Apaches had something in common. The Jivaro shaman had told him he must kill his enemies or they would destroy him. Worse. They would take his *arutam* spirit and leave him wandering in darkness forever. He could not allow that to happen. He had to kill his enemies first. He had to acquire their *arutam* spirits and make his own stronger. Make himself so strong that they would be afraid to kill him. That was the answer. To kill them. He had to....

"Steve. Steve!"

A hand was on his shoulder, the hand of the woman, the woman who was his enemy. With a snarl he grasped the hand and twisted it away and reached for the soft throat. She screamed and wrenched away, and he was thrown against the door of the machine as it rocked up on two wheels almost out of control.

"Jesus," he snapped, and grabbed the wheel to bring the car under control.

Her eyes swung from him to the road, her hands gripped the wheel hard, her face white. Oh, God. It had happened! He had lost control. He could have killed her. He fumbled the bottle of white pills from the glove compartment. Empty. Oh, Jesus. Could he keep from going completely mad without the pills? He dropped the bottle.

"Stop the car," he said.

Helen looked at him, fear pulling her face into harsh lines. She sped up. She was afraid that if they stopped he might kill her. But she was wrong. He would kill her if they didn't stop.

"Oh, God, Helen," he cried. "It's all right. I won't hurt you. Just please stop."

She swallowed and caught her lip between her teeth. Some of the fright had left her eyes. Then, on a straight stretch of the highway she was able to take a good look at his face. She moaned in anguish and brought the car to a stop at the side of the road. When Steve leaned over and shut off the engine she cringed away. He took the keys from the ignition and got out of the car. Her head twisted around to watch as he walked around to the trunk and opened it. Lying on top of his camping equipment was his blowgun, darts, and the butcher knife. A short length of rope was coiled atop some tire chains and pieces of junk. He reached for the rope and it alarmed him when his hand seemed to hover over the knife. With a groan he grabbed the rope and slammed the trunk lid shut. He got back into the car and handed the car keys and the length of rope to Helen.
"Here. I want you to tie my hands."

She made no move to take the rope. "But...why?"

Steve wanted to tell her. But then she would hate him and all her memories would be only of a crazy man, a murderer. But now he had to be sure that if he blacked out again he could not harm her. His head was pounding. Once they reached the reservation she could untie him and he would vanish from her life, leaving her only with memories of the man she knew as Steve Kelly.

"Do it," he demanded. "Just do it."

She studied his face and something collapsed within her. But she took the keys and the rope. Steve squirmed around in the seat and put his hands behind his back. He felt her slip the rope around his wrists and tie it.

"Tighter," he gritted. "Make it tight."

She did, and her tears dropped on his bonds. When she finished, she said with a strangled sob. "All right."

He turned away. "Now go. Fast. Make it fast."

She wiped her eyes with the back of her hand and started the car. She drove onto the highway and accelerated down the road.

Henry Warner wondered how it was possible to simultaneously wish that the Arizona Highway Patrol car would go faster and at the same time be terrified that it would. Beside him in the rear seat Irene Perez sat stiffly, swaying with the motion of the car as they rocketed along US 60 heading east from Phoenix, the siren wailing and the light-bar flashing. Like Henry, she was wearing hiking boots and blue jeans, only her jeans fitted her like those on the girl in the TV commercials. Her blouse was covered by a loose sweater and her long, lustrous hair was down and caught back with a shell-comb wound with a leather thong.

In the passenger side of the front seat Captain William Bell of the Arizona Highway Patrol put down the radio mike. His weathered face was pulled into a happy smile as he looked over his shoulder at Henry.

"That was the San Carlos police. They're setting up patrols on the western entrances to the reservation."

Henry had the impression that Bell enjoyed a high-speed chase. "They haven't seen him yet?"

"No, but he can't be too far ahead of us. That red Camaro was spotted out of Apache Junction just after we picked you up at the airport."

Irene turned from the window. "Was the blonde girl with him?"

"Can't say. At the time we weren't looking for him so nobody paid attention."

"He could have dropped her off anywhere," Henry said.

"In a way," Irene interjected, "I hope he didn't."

"Why?" Henry said. "Then she'd be safe."

"Because as long as she is with him he is still Steve Kelly."

"You think that if he turns into that headhunter he might try to kill her?"

"Yes."

"They're in love. Grady said they were thinking of getting married."

"I hope so," she said. "It might save her life."

Not giving in to pain does not mean it isn't there. Steve felt that if his headache got any worse he was going to start groaning. His entire body was drenched with sweat and he could feel darkness behind his eyes that required every ounce of his willpower to keep it from blotting out the sunlight. It felt like black acid eating through the walls of his brain. Behind his back his hands flexed and his muscles knotted, fighting the rope. He did not feel the pain of his lacerated wrists, nor the trickle of blood that ran down his hands.

Helen was staring ahead gripping the steering wheel like a vice, her body bathed in perspiration as she fought to control her anxiety. From time to time she glanced at Steve and when she saw his eyes rolled back and the drops of sweat beading his forehead, her eyes glistened with tears.

"Hold on, honey," she said. "We're almost there. We just passed the reservation entrance. Tell me when you want me to stop."

His eyes came into focus. "Soon," he said with an effort. "Another couple of miles."

His head tilted back and the blackness crept a little closer. The blood from his wrists made the rope slippery and one hand was almost free. Soon the machine would stop and he would be in the jungle. His blowgun, darts, and a knife were in the back of the machine. If he could find a shaman he would soon be free of the pain in his head. He hoped that his enemies would not try to stop him from finding the shaman. If they did he would have to kill them. For some reason that disturbed him. Why should killing his enemies make him uneasy? It was simply something that had to be done.

A mile ahead of the fast moving Camaro Sergeants Clark and Fowler, Apaches of the Reservation Police headed south on Highway 60. Sergeant Clark was using the radio.

"Understood. Ten-four." He replaced the mike. "Sounds like we've got a nut."

"Good." Fowler turned on the light bar and pressed down on the accelerator. "I hope the bastard tries something. I'm tired to giving tickets." *of*

Clark laughed. "Just remember, if we see him first I get to rescue the blonde."

The darkness moved in and retreated. And each time it stayed longer and was harder to force away. Behind his back the Jivaro's hands were almost free and he flexed them to restore the circulation. Now the woman could stop the machine and he would go find the shaman. What were the words to make her stop? He would think of them in a minute. Should he kill her? She was not an enemy. He decided that he would not kill her unless she tried to stop him.

He was about to wrench his hands from the slippery bonds when his eyes focused on another machine coming toward them. He had seen other machines pass them, but this one gave him a feeling of danger. It had lights on top that were blinking and it was moving at a great speed. That was the enemy. How he knew it, he was not sure, but he did know. The machine flashed past them. He turned his head to make sure they did not stop. But they did, their machine weaving and sending up a great cloud of white smoke. It skidded in a half circle and came after him. The machine made a high-pitched howl and he knew that the enemies inside were coming to kill him.

The woman saw the enemy too in the little mirror and she made their own machine slow down, so he snarled words he knew she would understand.

"No stop!"

She turned to him, fear in her eyes. "Steve," she said. "I've got to."

So she was an enemy! He shouted, "No!" and jammed his foot on top of hers on the pedal that made the machine go.

The woman tried to free her foot while clinging to the wheel. "Steve! No!"

They were going very fast, but the other car was gaining. He pressed his foot harder and yanked at his bonds. His bloody hands came free just as the machine of his enemies pulled even on their left side. He had to stop them before they got ahead where they would have the advantage. He grabbed the bottom of wheel and with a growl yanked it hard. The machine smashed into the machine with a sickening crash. The other machine slued sideways before it rolled and hurled through the air and off the road where it gouged up a geyser of dirt and rock, stopping on its side.

He'd taken his foot off the woman's and forced her against the door while he fought his own machine, almost bringing it under control as it skidded off the road and slammed into a tree, snapping his head forward so hard that his forehead smashed into the dash with stunning force. Steve opened his eyes. Why the hell had he done that? Christ! He was really in deep shit. If they caught him now they wouldn't wait for him to die; they'd hang him by the balls. Beside him Helen slumped over the wheel, sobbing.

"Helen?" he said. "I'm sorry. I'm sorry."

He reached for her and she cringed away from him. Oh, God. He had to find out about the men in the police car. The door on his side was stuck and he forced it open with a powerful kick and ran to the smoking police car. The car belonged to the reservation police and it sickened him to think what he had done. It would have been so easy if they'd left him alone. Then nobody would have been hurt. Well, it was too late to turn back now.

One of the policemen struggled out through a shattered window, blood coursing down his face from his forehead. Steve caught him as he slumped to the ground. The man reached for his pistol, but Steve snatched it from the holster. The policeman stared at him, anger burning away his fear. Steve could see through the pulverized windshield that the man who had been driving was unconscious or dead.

"What's your name?" Steve asked.

"Fuck you."

"Look, I don't want to hurt you." Steve pointed the gun at the policeman's head. "If you want to help your partner, you'd better cooperate."

"I'm Clark. He's Fowler. Let me call for some help."

"In a minute. First there's a couple of things I've got to do."

He motioned with the gun for Clark to walk ahead of him to the wrecked Camaro. Now that the emergency was past his headache was again shooting pain throughout his body and the darkness was descending like an evil curtain. No, not yet. Only a few minutes more. Then he would be free, where he could harm no one.

Helen was still sitting in the Camaro her head on her arms. She looked up when they approached, her eyes red and her face tear-streaked. Steve motioned for Clark to stand where he could cover him with the gun and yanked the door open.

"Helen," he said. "Are you all right?"

"I...think so."

He helped her out of the car and she stood, holding to the door. Keeping an eye on Clark, Steve reached in and pulled the keys from the ignition. He walked around to the back and unlocked the trunk. When he leaned in to reach his camping equipment his head was throbbing with such force he could scarcely focus his eyes. He put the gun down and Clark sprang at him with a grunt. He smashed Steve aside and tried to grab the gun. But Steve recovered his balance and grabbed Clark around the waist.

Clark swung his elbow against Steve's temple and he felt his brain explode in a flash of agony. With a scream of rage he lifted Clark and slammed him against the machine. Clark ripped at him with blows to the stomach and head, trying to drive the edge of his palm into Steve's throat. Steve thrust the man away. His enemy dove at him again with strange kicks that jarred his body, and Steve growled with a hate that was so powerful he stopped feeling the pain. He grabbed his enemy by the throat and lifted him off the ground and he could see the fear in the man's eyes as he struggled to breathe. Then the woman clawed at his arms and screamed. "No! Steve! No!"

Her stared at her, his face contorted with hate seeing pain and fear in her eyes. It was the woman from the machine. She had a name. Helen. Yes. That name was important. It meant something to him. Something he wanted to remember.   He said it.

"Helen."

"Yes, Steve! Let him go. Please."

He turned to look at the policeman whose face was purple, his eyes bulging. What the hell? He released—what was his name—Clark, who slumped to the ground gasping for air. He spun to face the woman. Was she his enemy? He did not think so, although she had stopped him from killing the policeman.

"Helen," he said, and his voiced sounded thick and ugly. "Get out of here. Go!"

She said, "Steve. Please let me help you."

He backed away. He did not want to harm her. But he could not let her stop him. He had to get away from this place before more enemies arrived.

She took another step and he reached into the open end of the machine and grabbed the knife. She stopped, her mouth parted, her breathing slowed. The pain was worse than ever, destroying the memory of why he was here and what he must do. He moved forward. Maybe she could tell him why he had come to this place.

She cowered away, her eyes on the knife. The knife. He could kill her so easily. Maybe then the pain would be over. Oh, God, no! He was going mad. That's what he had to remember. He was going mad. He had to run. Run for his life. Run away from the pain and the fear.

He grabbed his blowgun and darts and ran toward the trees. In the jungle he would find a shaman who could take the pain away. Then his enemies would never catch him.

The woman shouted, "Steve! Steve!"

But he did not stop; he did not see the man called Clark struggle to his knees and claw the gun from the trunk of the machine and aim it at his back. Nor did he see the woman grab the man's arm and shout just as he vanished in the forest.

Clark stared at the place where Steve had disappeared. Helen slumped to the ground and leaned against the rear fender of the Camaro sobs wracking her body. Clark staggered back to his car and looked at Fowler. He hoped to hell he wasn't dead. He reached in and clicked on the radio and keyed the mic. "Hello. Do you read? This is Clark. Do you read me?"

The radio crackled, and the dispatcher's voice said, "Clark? Where are you? Give your position."

"I'm two miles north of the Salt River Bridge. That madman wrecked our car. Fowler's hurt. How soon can you get here?"

CHAPTER 16

It had been years since Henry had enjoyed the tangy scent of pines and he promised himself he would make it a point to visit the mountains more often. Even the dreadful purpose of the journey failed to ruin his pleasure. Perhaps it was because Irene was with him. Like most people, he was proud of his country—or most of the things about it—especially its topographic diversity and he was glad that Irene was getting a chance to see some of the majesty of its snow-capped mountains, dense conifer forests, and rushing mountain streams. This area near Arizona's famous Mogollon Rim was among the most beautiful in the world. He would really enjoy exploring the Rim with her some time when images of death did not hover over them like winged gargoyles.

Captain Bell had parked where an ambulance and six official cars lined the shoulder of the road. Henry got out of the car and stood watching a knot of uniformed men who were examining an overturned reservation patrol car and a wrecked Camaro on the other side of the road. In the group near the Camaro was a blonde woman who he assumed to be Helen Kane. Thank God Kelly hadn't killed her. He had more than half expected that they would find her body.

Henry's muscles felt a little tight from the long confining ride, but when he held the door for Irene, she moved with her usual liquid grace. He noted that two reservation policemen were examining the ground between the Camaro and the trees as though they were looking at tracks. Damn. He hadn't wanted Kelly loose in the forest. He had pieced together a psychological profile from union files, and from talking to people who knew him, and from telephone conversations with the San Carlos reservation tribal officials. The profile added up to one tough *hombre* who was going to be hard to find, and even harder to capture. Not only had Kelly survived three years in the jungles of eastern Ecuador, but had spent his boyhood here on the reservation.

Of course, the reservation police also knew the country and they were just as anxious to get Kelly. The radio had said that the Apache policemen, Fowler, had died before the ambulance arrived. The other one, Clark, had cuts and bruises, but he was sure they all felt as though they had a personal vendetta.

They would keep after Kelly, no matter how long it took.

Even so, Henry was glad he had anticipated the possibility of Kelly's escape and had brought Irene with him. The Apaches might be noted hunters, but a couple of generations of reservation living might have softened them, dulled their instincts. And they sure as hell wouldn't understand the thought process of a Jivaro. Irene could tell them what Kelly was likely to do if anyone could. He walked with her and Captain Bell toward the men near the wrecked cars.

Bell said, "Hello Lee."

A wide-shouldered young man wearing the uniform of a San Carlos reservation policeman turned to them. He had hair as black as Irene's, but his skin was darker and the intensity in his deep brown eyes had the same warmth as looking into the muzzle of a double-barreled shotgun. Like the other Apaches, he carried a rifle.

"Lee," Captain Bell said. "This is Lt. Henry Warner of the LAPD. And this lady is Doctor Perez. This is Chief Lee Toga."

They shook hands and Bell told Lee Toga what Henry had said about Kelly.

Toga folded his arms, and stared toward the distant mountains.

"This man may be insane, but he killed one of my men." He nodded toward the two men who had been studying Kelly's tracks. "Phil and Carlos here are two of the best trackers in the world. I'll have six more in a few minutes. We'll have him before dark."

Bell said, "I can get you some help if you want."

Toga looked insulted. "We have jurisdiction here. We'll handle it."

Bell did not seem happy, but he shrugged. "Okay. You're in charge."

"We'd like to come along," Henry said.

Toga looked at Henry and Irene. "I don't think so. We'll be moving fast."

The way he said it made Henry wonder if it was because they would be in the way or because they might be witnesses. Irene studied the area silently with a deep frown.

"May I speak to the policeman who saw him run away?"

Toga looked at his watch with irritation. "Make it fast. We've only got a couple of minutes."

He led them to the people standing near the Camaro. Helen Kane was better looking than Henry had expected even though she had been crying and her hair was a mess. All the troopers were wearing clean uniforms except one. His was ripped and dried blood formed ugly blotches in several places.

"Clark," Toga said, and the man turned toward them. "How you feeling?"

Clark shrugged. "No big deal."

Henry was faintly amused. From what he had read of the Apaches they would have to be dead before they'd admit to being hurt. The man's pride certainly wouldn't let him admit anything short of a compound fracture.

"The lady has a couple of questions for you."

Clark assumed a carelessly alert stance that he must have practiced after watching old movies of Errol Flynn; or was it Clint Eastwood? "Sure. What do you want to know?"

"When he ran away, what did he take with him?"

Clark had to think a moment. "He didn't take the gun." He looked at Toga and his lips twisted into a smug grimace. "They usually forget things like that when they panic."

"He didn't panic," Helen Kane said. "He didn't want it. He didn't want to kill anybody."

Togo brushed the thought aside. "So what did he take?"

"Nothing except a plastic pipe and a knife."

"Only a knife," Toga said. "That'll make it easier."

Irene was alarmed. "He has the blowgun?"

"A blowgun?" Bell snorted. "And he left the pistol?"

A glance of amusement passed between the men as though to say that Kelly really was crazy.

Henry saw the look. "He's deadly with that thing."

Toga patted his rifle. "Ours shoot farther."

Helen took a step away from the Camaro. "He's not responsible.

He's sick. You can't kill him."

Toga's smile was chilling. "Don't worry. We're not going to do anything we don't have to."

"He just wants to find some...some medicine man. He thinks he can help him."

"We'll take him to the medicine man as soon as we get him." Toga turned away, and Henry saw Helen Kane's face collapse in grief. "Come on," Toga called to his men. "Let's get started. Clark, get in the ambulance. We've got to move."

"I'm going with you," Clark protested.

Toga studied Clark's defiant expression. "Okay. But we're not waiting for you."

"You won't have to."

Henry turned to Helen. "Miss Kane. You'd better go in the ambulance. We'll take it from here."

Helen's eyes searched his face. "Don't let them hurt him."

Irene took hold of Helen's arm and steadied her as they walked toward the ambulance. "They won't. He'll be all right."

"This guy's half Apache," Bell said. "Your guys might have trouble tracking him."

"Only half?" Toga's lips curled in a tight smile. "They'll have him in an hour."

Irene heard Toga's remark and turned to face him. "This man you are after, if he knows he is being followed, he will not be trapped. He will come to get you. You must be very careful."

Toga smiled at her with the reluctant tolerance of a professional listening to an amateur. "Ma'm," he said loud enough for the Apaches to hear. "These men are used to tracking wounded animals. They're not going to let themselves get boxed."

Irene shook her head. "You don't understand. Jivaros are different. Their entire lives are spent in hunting and being hunted."

Toga's smile was arrogant. "Okay, Ma'm. Thanks for the warning."

Henry piped up, "Well, if you're so sure it'll be that easy, why can't we come along?"

"Okay," Toga replied. "But if you can't keep up, we're not waiting for you."

"Fair enough."

Henry was not sure that Irene was in shape for hiking over rough terrain. For that matter, he wasn't ready for a triathlon himself. But if Toga was right they might not have to go far.

Toga and Tom Bell moved toward the two trackers. Irene watched them sadly. "If Steve Kelly really is Jivaro, many of them will die."

Henry looked at the tough, competent, heavily armed men. "I don't know. The Apaches are the greatest hunters in the world. A hundred years ago—"

"This is not a hundred years ago," Irene reminded him. "They are dealing with a people who have been hunting and killing one another for two thousand years."

Henry looked toward the forest where the two trackers had already vanished, and was glad he didn't have to go into the darkness. "He only lived with the Jivaros three years. I hope to hell he didn't learn too much."

Another reservation patrol car pulled up and six Apache policemen got out. All carried rifles in addition to their holstered pistols. From the trunk they brought out backpacks, which they strapped on. Lee Toga came over to Henry and Irene who were also shrugging into packs that had been provided by Tom Bell.

"We'll be moving out," Toga told them. "Try to keep up, please."

They walked fast. Following the file of Apache policemen Henry looked up at the blue sky through the fragrant trees and wondered how long it would be before they came down off this mountain and how many of them would stay—forever.

CHAPTER 17

The Jivaro became aware that he was being followed when he paused to survey his back trail. He waited motionless in the afternoon shadow of a huge Ponderosa pine while he fought to ignore the throbbing in his head. It was difficult to detect movement among the thick trees, but he knew what to look for: a flicker where there should not be a flicker, a bird startled into flight, or a flash of sun off a weapon or an article of clothing. He had discarded his own shirt, which had felt tight, unnatural.

There were two of them, and they were moving fast even though he had been careful with his trail. He would have to deal with them or they would lead the others to him. He was sure that they were people of this place, Apaches, and the thought gave him a vague uneasiness. Why should a reluctance to kill them pass through his thoughts? These were not his people—were they? No. They were not Jivaro. They were enemies and would have to be killed so he could search for the shaman who could stop the pain that radiated throughout his body.

It would not be easy. They had guns and would shoot him if they could. With his blowgun he could kill one of them, but the other might get him. He must think of a way to eliminate the first one, then he could use the blowgun on the other. He wished his enemies would stop putting darts into his head. The pain made it difficult to concentrate.

He moved up the slope keeping to the shadows and moving so quietly that not a branch was disturbed nor a pebble displaced. There were many traps that could be set to kill a man, but they required time and tools to build. He would have to find a natural trap.

He found what he was searching for as he moved along the rim of a deep ravine where a heavy growth of trees extended to the edge of the precipice. Huge boulders, many as large as houses, pushed against the trees. Instead of working his way around them he moved along the edge of the rim. He did not make the mistake of making his tracks obvious. That would cause them to suspect a trick. Even so, if they were as smart as they should be they would be cautious about following a trail so close to a natural kill zone. One of them would probably do the tracking while the other stayed inland away from the precipice, acting as a flanking guard. That is the way Jivaros would do it.

So he searched for the place he wanted. And when he found it he grunted in satisfaction. Here the drop was sheer to the floor of the canyon and the trees grew close to the edge, but not so close they would signal a trap. Behind the trees the huge jumble of boulders formed a natural barrier that would force the flanking guard toward the rim where he would have to move to a position where he would be visible behind the tracker.

The Jivaro noted all this while he was moving along the rim. He did not pause nor alter his path. A good tracker would detect the subtle change and suspect a trap. He continued along the edge of the precipice, past the trees, and around the ridge of rocks. Then he doubled his pace and circled to come into the trees from inland.

Moving carefully so he would not leave any sign for the trackers he selected a thick, chest-high tree limb that extended out over the cliff and stripped it of its branches. He then bent the heavy limb back so he could hold it while remaining concealed. In a *tambunchi* the bent branch would be fitted with spikes that would drive into a man's chest when the branch was released by a trip cord. But he had no spikes and no cord; he would have to hold the branch himself, although it put him in a very dangerous position.

Even though he had waited as long as was prudent before he bent the powerful branch back, his arms were grew weary as the lead tracker approached along the edge of the precipice. The man wore a kind of uniform that looked vaguely familiar, but more importantly, he carried his rifle carelessly in one hand.

He was a good tracker because he moved at a steady trot. But he had not tracked men before or he would have paused to examine the area ahead, which was a natural kill place. Instead, the man came on, his eyes on the ground. His panting could be heard as he worked his way up the slope along the rim of the canyon.

Then, just as the Jivaro had anticipated, the second man was forced by the boulders to come out of the trees, staying far enough back so he could keep an eye on his partner, but not so close that an ambush could take them. But they had already made their mistake and when the tracker reached the right position the Jivaro released the branch. It snapped with a swish. The tracker had such quick reflexes he was able to half turn and bring his rifle up before the branch swept him off the precipice. He made no cry as he plummeted far down to the rocks below.

The other man, moving with the speed of a jaguar, dove for cover as the blowgun dart caught him in the chest. He smashed to the ground and surged to his knees, clawing at the dart with both hands. He got to his feet and tried to locate his rifle. But he was losing control. He clutched at a tree as his legs refused to support him. Then the convulsions began and his breath rasped harshly while his arms and legs quivered. The life went out of his eyes, and except for muscular tremors, he was still.

The Jivaro moved to look at him. He wondered if he should take this enemy's head. He decided against it. There would be others following and he could not prepare the *tsantsa*. Later, when he had time, he would make substitutes for both men from the heads of wild pigs or other animals and placate their *arutam* spirits with a *hanlsamata*.

He debated about taking the gun. With it he could kill many enemies. But its noise would lead them to him. He would have a better chance if he killed them silently. So he picked the gun up and threw it far out over the cliff. He then stuffed leaves from an aspen tree in the mouth of the dead man, and turned the body face down so the man's *arutam* spirit could not get out and catch him before he had time to get away. Then he resumed his journey.

It was likely that more of his enemies would follow, but if he killed enough of them perhaps they would leave him alone. He was going to die soon. Somehow he knew that. But he would not be killed by these men. He also knew that.

CHAPTER 18

Under different circumstances Henry would have enjoyed the night. The air was fragrant, cool but not cold. There was no wind and the stars formed a vast canopy impaled on the tops of the towering pines. The firelight highlighting Irene's cheekbones made her look like an Inca goddess. Best of all, she was seated beside him, their backs against a fallen log, her side warm against his.

The mood was shattered when she turned to stare into the soundless darkness of the trees, and he felt her tremble. It wasn't because of the chill air; it was the Jivaro. He was out there somewhere. Late in the afternoon, when there had been no word from the two Apache trackers and the sun had slid behind the distant Sierra Anchas Mountains, they had set up camp for the night.

Captain Bell, Lee Toga, and the Apache policemen stood a few feet away talking in low tones as though they too were under the spell of the silent forest. Then Lee Toga and three of the Apaches separated from the group and trotted into the darkness.

Captain Bell spread his hands near the flames. "They're going to find Phil and Carlos. They should have been back by now."

Irene looked up at him, the firelight making her eyes appear to glitter. "If you find them they will be dead."

Bell's face tightened. "You think so?"

"I have told you. This man you follow, he is Jivaro. He lived with them; he thinks as they do. He will not wait to be killed."

"I can't believe he could take out both men. We didn't hear any shots."

Irene closed her eyes as though she were trying to control a strong emotion. "They are not here."

Bell thrust his hands into his pockets and stared at the fire. Like

Bell, Henry stared into the flames. He did not want to believe what Irene was saying. But he was beginning to and the thought was disturbing. Could this pseudo-Jivaro kill two trained Apache policemen without making a sound? Was he sitting out there waiting, planning how to kill those following him?

He looked up at the brilliant curtain of stars, each point of light as sharp as a stiletto. How could the beauty of such a night be connected with death? Maybe if the heavens were this visible in the city there would be less crime. Once again he promised himself that some day he would leave the city and live in a place like this. But not alone. It would have to be with a special woman.

He looked at Irene who was gazing into the flames. This was a special woman. She had not complained once all afternoon, even though much of the going had been over very rugged terrain.

"You know," Bell said, "the last great manhunt in the West was right around here."

Irene tilted her head and the firelight played with the smooth skin of her throat and face. "When was that?"

"Around the turn of the century. The last century."

"A hundred years." She looked back at the fire. "I am like most of the people of the world. I still think of your American West as being very primitive."

Henry thought of the vast wilderness around them and of the Apaches, Navajos, and Hopi who still roamed this wild country. "It still is in many way." He looked up at Bell. "You were thinking of the Apache Kid."

"The Apache Kid?" Irene nodded toward the reservation policemen who were building their own fire. "One of them?"

"One of their ancestors," Bell said. "He was a renegade even from his own people. Even the Apaches hunt in groups, especially when they make war. But the Apache Kid hunted alone. He killed about a dozen people, whites and Indians. They hunted him for years, but never caught him. He gave himself up once. But when he decided to escape, he and some other Apache prisoners killed their guards with their hands handcuffed. They never did capture him. And old scout named Huallapai Clark thought he wounded him and maybe he did. They never found out.

He just disappeared. Legend has it that he's still out there. Of course, that's nonsense. He'd have to be more than a hundred years old."

"It is possible," Irene said. "There are people living in the Andes who are well past one hundred years."

Henry looked toward the blackness beneath the trees. "Do you think Kelly can survive in this country? It's not much like the jungles of Ecuador."

"You told me he was Apache Indian. He grew up here. If he is able to function, he should be able to survive."

Bell licked dry lips. "What would you say was the effective range of one of those blowguns?"

"Fifteen meters. But I have seen them used at twice that distance."

"A hundred feet?" Bell whistled softly. "I figured about ten feet."

"He doesn't have to be too accurate," Henry reminded him. "The darts are poisoned. A hit anywhere on the body could be fatal."

Bell's hand sought the butt of his gun. "Jesus. I'll bet Mossman never had to deal with anything like this. I'd better tell everybody." He walked to the reservation policemen.

"Mossman?" Irene asked. "Who is this Mossman?"

Henry chuckled. "Nobody you'd know. He was head of the Arizona Rangers back when they were first organized."

"Arizona Rangers? You mean Texas Rangers."

"Texas wasn't the only place with rangers. The Arizona Rangers were just as tough."

"Oh." She looked toward Captain Bell and the Apaches. "I think it is good that your Indians are becoming more a part of your industry and government. I hope that ours will someday do as well. But I do not think so."

"No? Why not?"

"The people of the *Montaña* are so very different. Your natives may come from a different culture or different religion, but basically the way they think is, in the end, the way most men think; their values are the same. It is not so with our jungle Indians. They live in a dream world of ghosts and spirits. They move from one world to the other. They do so by using hallucinogenic drugs. They drink this *nateema* every day. In this way they are able to associate with the spirits of their ancestors. And their feuds last for generations. When a boy wakes up in the morning the first thing his father does is repeat to him a list of their enemies. The boy hears this every day and he knows that part of his life must be spent in seeking revenge against these enemies."

"Sounds effective. I wish the fathers of our kids would sit down with them every morning and tell them what is expected of them. Our kids have to pick up their morals on the street."

"My country is becoming like that. It is very frightening." She shivered and Henry got a blanket from his sleeping bag and put it around her shoulders.

She looked up at him. "Thank you. You are very gentle for such a strong man who carries a gun."

Neither of them noticed a movement in the dense shadows beneath the trees. The Jivaro stood for a moment studying the group. How many would he have to kill before they would go away? If he fired rapidly he could hit two before they would be able to use their guns. Which ones should he kill? The woman and the man beside her were the closest. It would be an easy shot. Those farther away would be more difficult. He might be able to kill the man and woman before the others noticed.

He raised the blowgun to his lips. The woman rested her head on the man's shoulder. He felt a vague memory of a woman's head on his own shoulder. Why should the thought disturb him? His forehead pulled into a frown as he watched the man put his arm around the woman. No. He did not want to kill them. They were not the most danger. It was the men with the rifles. He shifted his aim and fired.

Near the fire one of the Apaches coughed and put his hands to his throat. He fell to his knees clawing at the plug of a blowgun dart that protruded from the side of his neck. As he fell, kicking and twitching, the others stared at him in surprise. There was a sound like a watermelon being plunked. Another of the Apaches made an ugly sound and grabbed at his temple where a dart had buried itself to the plug.

The other Apaches and Captain Bell dove for cover whipping their rifles up to cover the trees. Henry was even faster. Perhaps it was because he was expecting it, but when he'd seen the first man fall he was seized by a chill. The Jivaro could kill Irene! He shoved her to the ground and covered her with his body, his gun in his hand, searching the darkness for a target. No one fired. Tom Bell and the Apaches rolled away from the fire and were lying behind any cover they could find, studying the trees. They were much too disciplined to fire at shadows.

The seconds ticked by. One of the Apaches rolled and in one fluid motion rose to his feet and sprang into the darkness beneath the trees. Another followed. One by one, Bell and the Apaches vanished into the dark forest.

Henry was deathly afraid that the Jivaro would kill him, leaving Irene an easy target. He kicked dirt on the fire, then rolled himself and Irene against the fallen log away from the dying light. He tried to hold his breath. He would not have been surprised to feel the sharp edge of a knife move across his throat or the needle-sharp pain of a blowgun dart. But there is no movement, no sound.

Irene whispered, "You are hurting me."

Henry realized that he was pressing the side of her face against the ground, and he released her while keeping her covered with his body. "Sorry," he whispered.

"It is all right. He is gone."

"How can you be sure?"

"The Jivaros are not fools. They kill as many as they can, then they go away so they will not be killed."

"Will he be back tonight?"

"I do not think so. By morning he will wish to be a long distance from here. That is when it will be most dangerous for him."

"I hope you're right." Henry raised his head and studied the forest. There was no sign of movement.

It was probably safe to release her, except that she felt so nice in his arms. Her cheek was almost under his lips and he successfully resisted the urge to brush it with a kiss. "But just in case," he whispered, "I'd better sleep with you."

She turned her face to an even more dangerous position with her lips almost touching his. In the darkness he could not make out her expression, but her voice was not shocked or angry, when she said, "Why, *Señor* Warner. You are most gallant. However, if I am going to lose something here on this wild mountain, it will probably be my life."

Henry's heart began beating faster. "Probably?"

She evaded the question by getting up. She stepped into the light of the dying fire and crossed to the bodies of the two Apaches. Feeling as vulnerable as a bait-goat Henry got to his feet and followed. He knew it was too late to help the Apaches. If Phil and Carlos were dead these two made four—five counting Fowler in the police car. At this rate they were going to run out of men long before they caught the Jivaro.

CHAPTER 19

As the first light of the sun cast a pale glow over the jagged mountains and thick forests below the Mogollon Rim, the Jivaro warrior stood on a ridge strewn with huge boulders and watched. Two Apaches slung their rifles across their backs and climbed down into the canyon toward the body of the tracker he had made go over the cliff. The other two at the top of the cliff were moving the body of the other man and studying the tracks and the tree branch, piecing together what had happened. In the still mountain air disturbed only by the chattering of bluejays he could hear one of the men at the top of the cliff talking into a small black box.

He watched until the men climbing into the canyon were well down the cliff, then he circled to approach the others from the lower slope. That was the path the four men had followed the night before and they would not expect him from that direction. It took him longer than expected because the pain in his head became so intense it made him dizzy, and he had to stop until the nausea subsided. But the pain helped because it was a reminder that these men were his enemies and he would never be free of their evil spirits until they were dead.

As he moved into position behind the two men he heard a strange sound. At first it was a throbbing beat and he believed it was coming from inside his head. But a high-pitched whirring noise was added to the beat. The sound seemed to be coming from down the mountain and he moved to a place where he could see better. Then he drew back in surprise. The sound was coming from a peculiar birdlike machine with a rotating thing on top and it was flying fast up the slope, following the contours of the canyon. When it was close enough he saw two men inside behind a large bubble of glass. One of the men was holding one of the black boxes close to his mouth and one of the men on the cliff was doing the same thing.

The flying machine circled and flew down close to the men in the canyon who were bending over the body of the dead enemy. The thundering noise echoed off the walls of the canyon, beating against his head like a thousand drums. The men inside the machine made it stand still in the air and they lowered a long basket to the men on the ground, who put the body inside. One of the men on the rim put his rifle down and both were watching the machine and the two men below. If he was quick the noise from the machine would cover any sound he might make.

It was easy for him to move close to the careless men and to shoot a dart into the neck of the one with the rifle. The other man was not even aware he was in danger until the one who had been shot fell over the edge of the cliff. The other man grabbed his rifle, but he was too late. The Jivaro, knife in hand, was closing on him.

The Apache dropped his gun, which clattered over the edge of the cliff, and caught at the Jivaro's knife hand, his impassive face tight with horror. For a moment he was able to hold the knife away, but with a quick wrenching movement, the Jivaro drove the knife into the man's side. The Apache gasped and doubled over. The Jivaro dropped his knife and lifted the man above his head and threw him out into the canyon. He fell down and down, slamming into a huge boulder in a twisted heap.

The men in the canyon stared up in stunned surprise. Then they unslung their rifles and shot at him. But it was a difficult angle and the bullets whispered past him. The flying machine dropped the rope leading down to the basket holding the dead man's body. Then the machine increased its noise and rose toward the top of the canyon.

The Jivaro picked up his knife and blowgun and moved back into the trees. The machine would be a danger. It could cover a great deal of ground searching for him. It would be very difficult for him to reach the river where he could find food and shelter without crossing cleared areas where the machine could see him. He would have to kill it.

But how? His blowgun and knife would be useless. And he did not have his enemy's rifles; they had gone over the cliff.

Hiding under the trees he studied the machine circling above him, the two men inside peering down. The machine was held up by the whirling thing on top. If he could destroy that whirling thing it should fall. He had to find a place where he could put his plan into effect.

Keeping to the concealment of the trees he trotted higher up the slope of the mountain. When he came to a place where the cliff changed to a steep, brush-covered slope he climbed down. The flying machine was still searching for him in the trees and he wanted it to come down into the canyon. He would have to make them see him.

He drew his knife and wiped the blade clean on the cloth of his pants. He angled the blade so the sun would cause a telltale glint. The men in the flying machine saw it and came fast to investigate flying down into the canyon. But he was already scrambling up to the rim keeping out of sight in the dense brush.

On the rim he turned and grunted in satisfaction. The machine was hovering below him, where he had been standing, while one of the men talked to his black box. It was a simple matter to pick up the six-inch thick trunk of a fallen tree and hurl it out and down like a lance into the whirling blades of the machine.

When the log struck there was a sharp crack followed by a splintering sound and the whirling blades threw off shards of metal. The sound of the machine's engine went up in a shrill crescendo and the machine flopped to one side and dropped straight down. It struck the brush and rocks on the slope and hesitated before it erupted with a flashing roar into a ball flames.

The thick ball rose from the canyon with an ominous smoke signal, followed by a thinner column of black smoke from the burning wreckage. With the horrible noise of the machine silenced the only sound was the faint crackle of flames. He could clearly hear one of the two men farther down the canyon scream. "My God!"

The other said, "Jesus! Who the hell is that guy?"

The first voice carried up the canyon. "I'm gonna get that son-of-a-bitch."

The Jivaro considered throwing boulders down on the two men, but far down the mountain there was a glint of sunlight on metal accompanied by the faint sound of voices. It was the main body of searchers. It would be best to put some distance between them and himself. He turned and trotted away.

It was becoming more difficult to move fast. He was terribly tired and the pain in his head caused him to double over retching. He had to find a place where he could rest. He remembered that on the other side of the mountain there was a narrow valley carpeted with trees. He would be safe there. Even if they brought more of the machines they would not be able to see him in the trees. He could rest there until he began the long journey down the far side of the mountain range to the distant river. The river. He had to reach it. It would be a good place to die.

CHAPTER 20

The morning matched Henry's mood: bright sunlight, and moody misty mountains. Perhaps it was the threat of dying that made him feel alive. Perhaps it was the joy of being in love and the awful depression of seeing the bodies of men who had died when they might have lived.

By the time the trackers led the posse over the crest of the final ridge and moved down into a narrow valley where they hoped to trap Kelly, Henry had made up his mind to ask Irene to marry him. He probably would have been better able to resist the nesting urge if he had been walking ahead of her instead of behind her. But for more than three hours he had watched the way her lovely body moved as she toiled up the slope and climbed over rocks and fallen logs. The times he helped her, tired as he was, the touch of her hand had given him a delightful surge of energy. Or perhaps it was because she had made the difficult ascent without complaint. The members of the group: two Apache reservation policemen, Captain Bell, and a reinforcement of eight state troopers, were maintaining a fast pace and Henry was hard pressed to keep up, so he knew how difficult it had to be for Irene.

Of course, nobody wanted to fall behind. By maintaining a tight formation like a squadron of bombers each gave protection to the others. The knowledge that stragglers would be the most likely targets kept everyone bunched up close to the leaders. The loss of the helicopter and the death of the best of the Apache trackers had cast a pall over the group and they moved silently clutching their rifles and scanning both sides of the trail.

As they started down a long slope into a picturesque valley that had steep rocky sides and a forested floor, a shadowy figure appeared in the trees to their left. One of the state troopers yelled and snapped off a shot as he dived for cover. In an instant the other troopers were firing and bullets shredded the limbs of trees and whined off boulders. Henry drew his gun and leaped to stand between Irene and the trees.

"Hold your fire! Hold it, Goddamn it!"

One of the Apache policemen yelled, "Hold it! It's Lee! Hold it!"

The firing died and as he stepped out from the protection of a large boulder, Lee Toga called again, "Hold your fire! It's me an' Charley."

Captain Bell echoed the command. "Hold your fire!"

When they could approach with a degree of safety the two Apaches left the shelter of the trees. "Take a break," Bell said, and the troopers flopped down on the carpet of pine needles.

Henry led Irene to a place where they could sit with their backs protected by a boulder. "Once again you have saved my life," Irene said, with a smile.

Henry grinned back. "I hope it doesn't get to be a habit."

Lee Toga said to Captain Bell, "We tracked him to the valley. He's not moving as fast as he was."

Bell checked his watch. "It's two o'clock. I've radioed for more men and a couple'a more choppers. But I doubt they'll get here before tomorrow. That means we've got to spend another night."

"Unless we get him today."

"How the hell are we gonna do that? We aren't gonna catch him by walking around in a bunch and if we don't, he's gonna pick us off. We've got to get more men."

The Apaches glanced at one another, their pride stung. Henry was glad he didn't have to live up to a brave warrior image. It wouldn't damage his ego to stay in the middle of a group and wait for reinforcements.

Lee Toga looked at the clear blue sky. "We aren't waiting. We're going after that son-of-a-bitch."

Bell wiped his hand across his mouth and turned away. "I can't order you to wait. I have no authority over you. But I think you're being very foolish."

Irene whispered, "He should not have said that. Now they will have to go."

"Yeah. I don't think he's much of a psychologist."

Lee Toga beckoned to Irene. "Dr. Perez, would you come here a minute?" Henry helped her to her feet and they went to join the group. "Doctor, you know the ways of this man. If we made him think we were going away, what do you think he would do?"

Irene pursed her lips. "Well, we know he is in much pain. He believes the pain is made by the spirits of his enemies. So if he thinks he is not being pursued, he will try to find a place where he can prepare substitute *tsantsa* and—"

"*Tsantsa?*" Charley asked.

"The head of his enemy," Irene explained. "To a Jivaro the soul lives in the head. If he does not take the head after he has killed an enemy, he can make a substitute. I believe he will try to find a place where he can do this as soon as possible."

"What kind of a place?" Lee Toga asked.

"A place where he feels he will be safe in the open. I think it will be near water. He does not have the canteens as we have. He will have to find water."

"This valley heads off toward the Salt," Charley volunteered.

"Yeah," Lee agreed. "Chances are he'll take the easy route along the floor if he thinks he isn't being followed. We'll make it look like we're pulling back. Then we'll circle around and set up an ambush where it narrows at the other end. When he comes out, we'll get him in a crossfire."

"Sounds good," Bell said, and the others murmured.

But Irene looked skeptical. "I do not think he will walk into your trap. He will know you are there."

Lee Toga would have smiled if not for the fact that five of his friends were dead. His voice was flat when he said, "He won't know we're there." He turned to Captain Bell. "You pull back down the mountain. We'll go along with you a ways, then we'll break off and start our move. Hawk, you go with Charley. Quirt, you come with me."

As they picked up their gear, Henry said, "I hope you don't have to kill him. He's sick, you know."

Lee checked the action of his rifle. "I'd hate like hell to meet him when he's well."

Henry could almost read Toga's mind. The Apaches were caught in an ugly situation. It didn't matter at this point whether more of them died; it was important that they prove their courage. They had to kill Kelly or be killed. It was useless to pursue the matter.

Henry walked beside Irene as they started the journey back. "You don't think it'll work?" he said.

She shook her head. "*Quien sabe.* It will depend on how much Jivaro he is and how close he is to dying. If he is truly Jivaro and if he is not close, then more of them will soon be dead."

CHAPTER 21

It was thirst that made the Jivaro turn away from his enemies, move over the crest of the mountain, and retreat down the far side. It was too soon to end his observation; it was unnatural for his enemies to give up the pursuit. But they were going away because he had killed so many that they were afraid of him. They might even believe that he was kararam and could not be killed.

He studied the valley, which he knew was the most direct route to the distant river called Salt. He did not like the valley. It was the kind of place he would choose for a trap: wide in the middle and narrow at the far end. Brush and stunted trees clung precariously to the rocky walls. In a clearing near the center of the valley was the ruin of an ancient log cabin, the thatched roof partially collapsed. The valley floor was flat and it would be easy walking, but dangerous. He would prefer to stay on the ridges where he could see his enemies without them seeing him. But he was already very weak. Perhaps there would be water near the ruins of the cabin. He had to quench the fire that burned in his head and inflamed his body. More and more often he was forced to pause and wait for the pain and sickness to pass. He had to take a chance.

When he reached the tree-covered floor of the narrow valley it was partially in shadow cast by the afternoon sun. Keeping to the concealment of the trees, he moved swiftly. Near the ruins of the cabin he stopped. He had been right; there was a spring. He could see the water seeping up in a green patch near the rotting logs that formed the sides of the cabin. He squatted on his haunches and studied the area. If he went for the water he would have to cross the clearing. He would be in view of anyone on the rim of the valley. Except that his enemies had gone away. Still, it could be a trick. They could be watching the water, guessing that he would try for it. But he had no choice.

With a grunt of frustration he surged to his feet and ran as fast as he could across the clearing to the spring. It would be a long rifle shot from the rim of the valley and he was a difficult target. To his relief, there were no shots. Maybe they had gone away. He drank quickly and deeply, the cold water caressing his parched throat. But it did not take away the pain in his head. He was not surprised. Water could not stop the darts his enemies were throwing into his brain. And the darts were getting stronger. He must find a place for the hanlsamata soon or it would be too late.

He trotted into the shadows of the trees and hurried toward the narrow mouth of the valley. Here was the place of most danger. Only a fool would go out of the valley between the two boulder-strewn ridges. He should climb the steep side and follow the rim. But he was weak and time was short. There had been no sign of his enemies when he was at the spring. He would have to take the chance.

He moved with increasing caution into the narrowing pass keeping to the shadows as much as possible. Through the narrow opening of the canyon mouth he could see the flat, tree-covered plain leading to the distant river. It was a powerful magnet that made him want to rush forward. He had already taken a step when he stopped beside a huge pine. Something was wrong. He could feel it.

He stood motionless, testing the environment with his senses. What was it that had made him stop? He could detect nothing out of place. He was close to the narrowest point at the mouth of the valley and a breeze was blowing toward him from the river. It would get stronger as the day grew shorter until it died at nightfall. Perhaps some false sound had been borne to him by the breeze. He listened poised, ready for flight, ignoring the pain in his head. This was the best place for an ambush. His enemies could have circled and moved ahead of him if they were very fast and in good condition. Then all they had to do was wait in the shadows for him to pass below them.

Pain shot through his head of such strength that he felt a new wave of hate. He had to stop the darts before the pain made him crazy. He almost hoped that his enemies were waiting. Except that he had to reach the river. The nausea of intense pain drove away his caution and he started forward.

He stopped. It was there; the thing that had made him stop. Not a sound. An odor. It came from a man; shaving lotion. He was right. His enemies were ahead of him, waiting.

Slowly he back-tracked. It was hard going, but he climbed the steep side of the valley to the ridge. They would not expect him above them. He moved carefully through a jumble of house-sized boulders flanked by pines and aspen. Then he saw a shadow on the slope below that did not blend with the others. He watched it until his eyes sorted out the shape of a man lying prone in shadows on the top of a huge boulder with his gun trained on the valley floor. The man would not be alone.

The Jivaro searched until he discovered another man crouched behind a fallen tree, aiming his rifle through the screen of branches. From the valley floor he would never have seen them until too late. He searched for other enemies, but there were only the two. The others must be on the opposite side of the valley. The remaining members of the group would be up along the ridge where they would be waiting for the sound of shots before they moved in. So, if he killed these two quickly the way would be open to the river.

He lifted his blowgun and drifted down the slope. But he was not silent enough. The man on the rock grunted and swung around. His rifle was coming up when the blowgun dart struck his chest with a sound like a hand slapping cloth. It was not a good shot. There had been no time to aim and the man was able to stand and fire one shot before he slumped off the boulder to writhed on the ground while the sound of the shot echoed along the walls of the valley.

Startled, the other man swung around and fired in one fluid movement. But the shot was defensive and the bullet slashed into a tree several feet from the Jivaro. The man levered another round into the chamber. He had spotted his target and the muzzle of the gun was swinging into line when the Jivaro's blowgun dart smacked into his forehead. The man's trigger finger squeezed reflexively and the gun bucked out of his hands, but the bullet hit the Jivaro high up on the left leg.

His body was already so saturated by pain it was difficult to distinguish a new one. He only knew he had been hit because the impact of the bullet almost knocked him down. As he turned to go a sharp agony lanced through his leg and it almost collapsed. There was no time to examine the wound; the others would already be on their way to investigate the shots. But if he was bleeding heavily he would not get far before he collapsed.

He sat down and used the knife to cut away the cloth of his pants from around the wound. He grunted with relief. The fully-jacketed bullet had gone straight through the heavy muscles of his thigh without making much of a hole. There was bleeding, but it was not excessive. He tore strips of cloth from the pants leg and bound the wound. The bandage would hinder his movement, but it would prevent leaving a trail of blood that would lead his enemies to him.

He picked up the blowgun and stood with an effort, debating whether to go after one of the rifles. The wound reduced his mobility. But if he had a rifle he could kill at long range. He would have to take a chance. He hobbled down the slope toward the twisted bodies of the two men.

He had taken only a few painful steps when he heard other enemies approaching at a run. He might be able to make it to the guns, but if he failed he would be caught in the open. He turned and started up the slope and a wrenching pain buckled his leg. Again he tried to climb the slope and again his leg refused to support him. He was unable to get up to the safety of the ridge; he would have to work his way down into the valley. But with the exit blocked it was a trap where he could be hunted down.

Maybe that was the answer. The enemy would never expect him to go there. If he could make them think he had slipped through the pass and was headed for the river, they would not search the valley. He could hide until it was night. Then he could make it to the broad river plain where they would never find him.

Moving as fast as he could he worked his way down the slope and angled toward the mouth of the canyon. When he was sure the trackers would believe he was heading for the river, he reversed direction, and keeping to the heavy growth, eased away from the ambush spot back into the valley. As he moved, he heard the men on the slope. One of them had already picked up his trail and shouted that he had found blood.

"Now we'll get the bastard," another man said. "He's heading for the river just like we figured."

Moving back up the valley the Jivaro took care not to leave tracks. Even so, a good tracker could follow if they decided that he had not gone toward the river. But that would take time. All he had to do was stay hidden until darkness.

His plans came crashing down with the sound of a shot and the slap of a bullet into a tree trunk. His enemies! They had to be the main group he had seen back down the mountain. They had hurried back faster than he had anticipated. In the daylight, he would never be able to work his way past them. And the shot would bring the others back from the mouth of the valley. He was trapped between the two forces. He had to find a place to hole up where they could not kill him before he could escape in the darkness.

The old cabin! Even if they knew he was there, they would not be able to take him. He had several darts remaining. He could keep his enemies at bay until night, then they would never find him. Taking advantage of every bit of cover, he moved as rapidly as possible. The door had fallen inward so he was able to enter quickly, certain that he had not been seen. He was wrong.

There was the crack of a shot from far up the canyon and a bullet struck the side of the cabin. His enemies were too far away for accurate shooting, so he took his time wedging the door in place. Using logs fallen from the collapsing roof, he propped the door so it could not be forced open.

He surveyed the single room. There were gaping windows on three sides as well as holes in the walls where the chinking had fallen out from between the logs. Good. He could cover all sides with his blowgun. *the*

In the middle of the dirt floor he cleared away some of the dry grass that had fallen from the sagging roof and sat down. He was more tired than he had ever been in his life. But he must not sleep. He allowed the terrible pain in his head to wash over him. For him there would be no sleeping, not for a long time.

A short distance up the valley Tom Bell motioned for his men to spread out. He had seen the madman go into the old cabin and he smiled. "We've got him now," he said to Henry and Irene.

Henry studied the ravaged cabin set in a clearing. "Except for one thing; who's going to go in after him?"

Irene added, "He is like a cornered animal. He will be very dangerous."

Bell nodded. "He's got the advantage. It'll be damn hard to take him."

"Why even try?" Henry asked. "He's wounded. All you have to do is wait him out. He can't get away."

Lee Toga came trotting through the trees. "Did you see him? He's in the cabin."

"Yeah. I got a shot at him, but it was too damn far."

"Charley's covering the other side. We've got the bastard now."

Tom Bell said, "It'll be dark soon. That might be what he's waiting for."

Toga spat on the ground. "We hit the son-of-a-bitch. He can't get away."

Irene asked, "Where was he hit?"

Toga made a grimace. "Don't know. We found some blood. Maybe he's hit bad."

Henry tried to remember the way the Jivaro had moved in the clearing. "I think he was limping. But he was quick enough when he jumped inside."

Tom Bell's voice reflected his frustration. "Well, I'm not going to risk any more men." He swung his arm, and called, "Surround the cabin. Stay out of range of that blowgun. Use your rifles. Wait for my signal."

Irene caught his arm. "No. All you have to do is wait. He's too sick to get away."

Some of the fire went out of Bell's eyes. "I'm sorry. I can't take the chance."

Irene stared at him, fatigue and hopelessness shadowing her face. "You intend to kill him. Isn't that right?"

"No. If he wants to surrender, we'll take him into custody."

Irene shook her head. "He'll never surrender. Never."

Toga's eyes mirrored sarcasm. "You want to go in after him?"

Spots of color appeared in her cheeks. Henry felt a surge of anger. What the hell was Toga trying to do, shame her into an admission that she was wrong, that the life of the madman was not worth risking anyone's life? It was an underhanded tactic Toga was using to put her in her place. He did not realize that her sense of pride was as strong as that of any Apache. Toga had made it impossible for her to back down. Damn the man.

"Yes," she said. "I will talk to him."

She took a step toward the cabin and Henry caught her arm. "No, he'll kill you."

She stared at the old cabin as though fascinated by the waiting death. "Not if he thinks I'm not a threat." There was no conviction in her voice.

Henry stomach knotted. "How do you know what he thinks? He's insane."

Irene shrugged away from his grip. "I've got to try."

She drew a shuddering breath and Henry realized that she was very much afraid. But she was also determined. His fear made him do something incredibly foolish.

He said, "No. I'll go."

That maniac in the cabin would put one of those darts in his neck as soon as he got close enough and that thought clutched at his gut. Maybe if he was fast enough he could see the dart coming and duck aside. It would take incredible reflexes, but maybe, just maybe it could be done. Besides, there was no way he could avoid going now. He might be able to lose face in front of the men, but he could never back down in front of Irene. How many men had been killed because the fear of death was less terrifying than the fear of appearing a coward in the eyes of a woman? What was that old saying? *Stupidity may get you into trouble, but it is pride that keeps you there.* Well, now you could add one more *estupido* to the list.

Irene moved in front of him. "Wait," she said. He hoped she had changed her mind. "He will surely kill you. He might not kill a woman."

His faint sense of hope drained away. "'Might' isn't good enough."

He moved her aside and she put her arms around his neck, holding him with a desperate energy. "No, Henry. Please."

Suddenly, Henry wanted to live more than he'd ever wanted anything in his life. The concern, the love in her voice, in her eyes, was there for him and he was filled with an awful uncertainty. There was the insane pleasure at knowing that she cared about him and at the same time the fear that he had to go? Reluctantly, he disengaged her arms. "Don't worry. I'll be back."

She clutched at his arm. "Together. We'll go together."

He licked his lips wondering if there might not be a way to save them both. Maybe there was enough of Steve Kelly left in the Jivaro that he would not kill them if they approached him together. He would surely see that they were not coming to kill him. Wouldn't he? The odds were better than if either one of them went alone.

"Okay. Maybe it'll work."

Lee Toga said, "Forget it. That son-of-a-bitch isn't worth it."

He raised his rifle and began shooting at the wooden door as fast as he could lever cartridges into the chamber. To Henry, the sound of the shots rolling off the walls of the valley was like the voice of God. It meant that neither Irene nor he had to die. Now it was out of their hands. He closed his eyes so that Irene would not see his relief. The other troopers began firing and gouts of dust, dirt and wood exploded from the rotting logs.

Inside the cabin the Jivaro rolled against the base of a wall with the first shot and peered through a chink in the logs near the floor, his blowgun ready. But none of his enemies were close enough. They were going to stay well back and hope to hit him with a lucky bullet. And it would have to be very lucky. The lower logs were relatively intact and as long as he remained close to the floor they could shoot until their ammunition was gone. Then they would be his.

Henry watched the firing for a moment. He doubted that the Jivaro would be hit.

He told Bell, with resignation, "You're not going to get him that way."

"The hell we won't. Nobody can live through that."

Henry turned to Irene and shrugged. The troopers were like sharks at a feeding frenzy. There was no way he was going to stop them.

After a minute, Henry said, "What happens when you run out of ammunition?"

Bell said, "My men are damn fine shots. He's probably dead already."

"If he is dead, go bring him out."

Bell's jaw tightened. He looked at Toga who was levering another cartridge into the hot chamber of his rife. Toga lowered the rifle and waved his arms.

"Cease fire! Cease fire!"

The firing stopped in a ragged cadence, the last echoes rolling down the canyon.

Toga swept his arm forward. "Move in."

Toga and Bell took a couple of steps forward and stopped. None of the men moved. Henry didn't blame them. They might be the greatest shots in the world, but they were trying to hit a target they couldn't see. And those who went to check the results might not come back.

Toga fingered his rifle as though he wanted to order the firing to begin again. But he couldn't do that. All his men and the state troopers were waiting for him to make the first move. He took a step toward the cabin and sweat popped out on his forehead. He took another step. Then he squared his shoulders and began walking.

Irene said, "Wait." Toga stopped as though someone had jerked him with a rope. "If he isn't dead, he'll kill you."

Toga stared at the cabin as though hypnotized. "I've got to find out."

"No you don't," Captain Bell said. "I know a way to make sure."

Toga looked at Bell. His face was as impassive as ever, his eyes flat, but everyone knew he was damn glad for the interruption that had prolonged his life.

"What's that?"

"Fire."

Toga's face came alive at once. Turning, he called, "Charley. Give me a hand. Get some of those dry branches."

He took his knife from its sheath and cut an aspen sapling and began trimming away its branches. Charley ran to help him, circling well away from the cabin. He began gathering short lengths of tinder dry pine branches.

Watching them, her face pale, Irene said, "No. Oh, no."

Henry had felt a slow horror building. He'd always had a repressed fear of fire and the thought of using it as a weapon cut through his fear with a swift anger.

"You don't want to do this. Not with fire."

Bell didn't take his eyes from the cabin. "If he's dead, it won't matter. If he isn't, it'll smoke him out."

Irene's voice had the strength of rage. "He will not come out. He'll never surrender."

Henry was filled with a familiar numb despair. "Ah, what the hell, I'll find out."

Lee Toga said, "Stay back."

Then he ran a zigzag pattern toward the cabin. In his hand was a makeshift lance tied with a bundle of blazing pine boughs. When he was close enough to the cabin, he pulled his arm back to throw.

Thwack! The sound of the dart hitting his chest reverberated in the still mountain air. Toga flinched and his arm came down. Then he pulled himself up again. *Thwack!* Another dart sank into his chest.

Toga's shrill scream of defiance echoed off the canyon walls, and he threw as he fell. It was not a good throw. The blazing lance wobbled in a high parabola and landed flat on the rotting roof of the cabin. The string holding the burning twigs burst, scattering them. Instantly there was a puff of smoke and flames began to lick at the dry grass and timbers.

Henry pulled Irene back into his arms and, as Lee Toga convulsed in the familiar dance of death, he heard her murmur, "*Matre de Dios.*"

The troopers and Apache policemen stood unmoving as the flames spread across the tinder-dry roof of the cabin and down the logs of the sides. No one made a move to reach Lee Togo. There was no point in joining a dead man.

Henry stood with his arms around Irene, staring at the flames and billowing smoke. "He's got to come out," he muttered. "He's got to."

He felt Irene shiver. "I hope so," she said. "But I don't believe it."

Inside the burning cabin, the Jivaro stared at the flames in more anger than alarm. His muisak soul would surely perish in the smoke and fire. For a warrior, it was not a proper way to die.

The roof was now a seething inferno. He moved around the small room searching for a place to escape the flames. But there was none. Even the tinder-dry walls were sheathed in writhing flames and the heat was like the inside of hell. Each breath seared his lungs. He felt his hair singe and curl, then burst into flame and he clawed at it in a frenzy of pain and rage. He could feel the skin of his face, his shoulders and back blister and peel. This was not the way for a warrior to die!

He raised the blowgun and screamed defiantly at his enemies. He would not die! He would not die!

Drawing his knife he dug frantically at the dirt of the floor while the flesh of his body burst into blisters and sloughed away in the horror of the fire.

CHAPTER 22

Henry and Irene sat on a fallen log and stared across the clearing at the smoldering remains of the cabin. The sun, seen through a lingering haze of smoke, was a blood-red ball balanced on the horizon, the long shadows of the trees like reaching fingers. Since the ugly crackling of the flames had died, there had been no sound, not a bird, not an insect. It was as though an evil spell had settled on the valley with a presence that was tangible.

The state troopers and Apache policemen felt it, too. When the flames had begun to consume the old cabin they had shouted defiantly, waiting for the Jivaro to come out and surrender, joyous that no more of them would die. But as the flames mounted and the Jivaro did not appear they realized that he had chosen to die in a manner reserved for nightmares, and their voices died. Even the evening breeze had stopped as though it too was holding its breath, waiting for the soul of the Jivaro. By the time the roof and walls collapsed the silence was broken only by the murmur of men praying to their own gods.

Henry stole a glance at Irene. She was staring sadly at the ruins of the cabin. The rays of the setting sun breaking weakly through the haze of smoke had turned her golden skin into magnificent bronze polished to a warm luster. Her lips were slightly parted and her eyes were lustrous by a mist of tears.

Henry put his arm around her shoulders and she leaned against him like a child seeking comfort. God, why did such joy have to be born in such tragedy? He touched her hair and when she half-turned to look at him, his mouth was drawn to her warm lips. At first her lips retreated and her breath was a soft gasp. Then they moved forward to seal with his own and Henry felt a wild joy.

His voice trembled when he asked, "Do you have to go back?"

"Yes," she said softly. "But I do not have to stay."

Henry began to smile. She reached out and touched his cheek with fingers as delicate as tears.

Captain Bell had been sitting on a fallen log, his face drawn into lines of sorrow and guilt. He looked as though the last few hours had taken years from his life. He stood up wearily.

"It's getting dark," he said. "Let's go."

He walked past the body of Lee Toga, moving purposefully, a man looking for the face of death. The other men also began moving, their eyes fixed on the ruins of the cabin, their rifles poised, as though expecting to feel the bite of a poisoned dart at any second.

Irene stood up, and Henry touched her arm. "You'd better not go. It's not something you should see."

"I've got to know," she said, and began walking.

Henry walked beside her. He was not looking forward to seeing the body. He had seen many kinds of violent deaths, but thank God, never the blackened body of death by fire. He was definitely not going to like this.

Bell and the others arrived at the cabin. They peered into the interior past the smoldering logs standing at the base of the walls. The earthen floor was covered with a layer of ash. There was no odor of burned flesh, no mounds that might have been a body. Everything had been consumed in the terrible blast-furnace heat of the fire.

Bell used the toe of his leather boot to test the ashes. "Seems cool enough."

He stepped into the ankle-deep ash and began a slow walk, placing each foot reluctantly, his face showing revulsion at what he might encounter. The other men joined him. Irene and Henry also stepped into the layer of ash, searching for any sign of the Jivaro's body. One of the Apaches grunted and held up a melted, twisted length of plastic conduit.

"Look at this. Must have been his blowgun."

"Hey!" the Apache called Charley said. "We got the stinger out of the bee."

"Yeah," one of the troopers said, with a grin. "The son-of-a-bitch wouldn't run off without it." He looked at Irene, his smile strained. "Would he?"

Irene shook her head. "No. He would not leave it."

Now everyone smiled. They straightened as though they had been instinctively hunched to escape an expected blow. Back and forth they moved across the ash-covered floor, their steps slowing. Bell finally stopped and looked at Henry and Irene, his forehead pulled into lines of worry. "He isn't here."

"He's got to be," Henry said. "You had the place surrounded. He never came out."

"So where the shit is he?"

The Apaches looked at one another, their faces drawn and pale. The troopers eyes lifted as though they to began believing that the Jivaro had turned into some kind of evil spirit that might strike at any second.

"Look again," Henry said. "He's got to be here."

He stepped forward to make the point, using his foot to sweep at the ashes. Irene was near the center of the cabin and she gasped as she felt the earth tremble. Henry turned in time to see her look at her feet. Her mouth opened as a hand like a claw shot out of the earth and fastened on her ankle. She shrieked, the ugly sound tearing from her throat as the earth erupted and a nightmare emerged.

It was an apparition from the bowels of hell. The skin of the face and the hairless skull was an oozing mass of blisters and clinging dirt, the eyes bulging, burning like living coals, the shreds of lips pulled back from white and shining teeth. The creature let go of Irene and rose to its full height with chunks of earth falling away from the burned and oozing flesh. It lifted one arm, a knife clutched in a fist of exposed bones and tendons.

Henry was the first to move. His pistol was out and firing as he leaped forward. He saw the bullet strike the creature in the chest and it jerked backward. The thing made a guttural sound and the knife came down in a vicious swing, but Henry had already yanked Irene aside as he fired two more shots into the creature and it dropped the knife with a gurgling cry.

Then its talon-like fingers were around Henry's neck and his nostrils were clogged with the sickening odor of burned flesh and he eyes were locked on the horror that had once been a face. But the hands on his throat had no strength and he brought his own arms up inside and knocked them away. The thing lost its balance and teetered back on legs that were shreds of flesh and white bones.

Before the creature could recover, a rifle cracked and a section of the face disintegrated. Then another rifle cracked and another and another until the valley was rocked with an echoing roar, the bullets carrying away slabs of rotting flesh and bone. The thing made another gut-wrenching sound, but it did not fall. It spread its arms, and as the bullets tore at its flesh and bone, it drew within itself as though it was fighting even this last desperate battle alone.

Then it fell, backward, what was left of the face turned to the last rays of the sun. The firing stopped, the echoes rolling down the valley as though carrying the soul of the Jivaro with it. The thing on the ground gave a last sigh and seemed to meld with the smoldering earth.

Henry took off his jacket smeared with the stench of the creature and dropped it over the horror that had been a face. The men stood silent, staring at the thing. No one came close. Even Captain Bell stayed back.

Henry looked at them. "We should bury him."

The men shifted. "I won't touch it," one of them said, and the others nodded.

Henry looked at Bell. "What about you?"

Bell licked dry lips. "I guess I could help."

Irene shook her head. "No. Leave him." She looked around at the beauty of the valley. "This place is a fitting grave."

One of the Apaches said, "No Apache will ever come to this place. Let it be his."

He turned and led the way to the body of Lee Toga. He and one of the other Apaches picked it up and began the long walk out of the valley.

Captain Bell took one last look at it. "I sure as hell wouldn't want to come back here day or night." He dropped the Jivaro's twisted blowgun next to the horror and walked away.

Irene looked to the blue sky and the green of the trees, and drew close to Henry. "He must have been Jivaro. Only a *kararam* could have so much power that he could not die."

"Maybe," Henry said. "But he was once a man named Steve Kelly. The poor bastard; what the hell did he ever do to deserve this?"

He put his arm around her shoulders and they walked out of the terrible valley, leaving it to the soul of the Jivaro.

The End

Printed in the United States
1252000006B/73-99